Dark Dragon's Mate

(Darkwing Dragons Book 1)

Anastasia Wilde

Copyright © 2019 Anastasia Wilde

All rights reserved.

ISBN: 9781091371163

No part of this book may be used, reproduced, stored in a retrieval system, or transmitted in any form or by any means, electronic or mechanical, including photocopying, recording, scanning, uploading, or distributing via the internet, print, or any other means, without written permission from the author.

This book is a work of fiction. The names, characters, places, and incidents are products of the author's imagination or have been used fictitiously, and are not to be construed as real. Any resemblance to persons, living or dead, actual events, locales or organizations is entirely coincidental. The author does not have any control over and does not assume any responsibility for third-party websites or their content.

Published in the United States of America.

Cover design by Melody Simmons

Books by this Author

Silverlake Shifters Series:
Fugitive Mate
White Wolf Mate
Tiger Mate

Silverlake Enforcers Series:
The Enforcers: KANE
The Enforcers: ISRAEL
The Enforcers: NOAH

Bad Blood Shifters Series:
Bad Blood Bear
Bad Blood Wolf
Bad Blood Leopard
Bad Blood Panther
Bad Blood Alpha

Wild Dragons Series:
Dragon's Rogue
Dragon's Rebel
Dragon's Storm

Darkwing Dragons Series:
Dark Dragon's Mate
Dark Dragon's Wolf

CONTENTS

Chapter 1	1
Chapter 2	7
Chapter 3	11
Chapter 4	16
Chapter 5	23
Chapter 6	33
Chapter 7	39
Chapter 8	46
Chapter 9	51
Chapter 10	58
Chapter 11	64
Chapter 12	70
Chapter 13	79
Chapter 14	84
Chapter 15	89
Chapter 16	95

Chapter 17	101
Chapter 18	107
Chapter 19	113
Chapter 20	119
Chapter 21	126
Chapter 22	134
Chapter 23	142
Chapter 24	148
Chapter 25	155
Chapter 26	160
Chapter 27	168
Chapter 28	173
Chapter 29	181
Chapter 30	187
Chapter 31	194
Chapter 32	198
Chapter 33	200
Chapter 34	207

Chapter 35	212
Chapter 36	218
Chapter 37	226
Chapter 38	230
Chapter 39	237
Chapter 40	243
Chapter 41	249
A Note from Anastasia	255
About the Author	257

CHAPTER 1

Trish didn't know which was going to hit her first—the thunderstorm or the uncontrolled Change.

She glanced up at the night sky, heavy with dark, threatening clouds. Thunder rumbled overhead. Inside, her wolf growled.

Out, she was saying over and over. *Out out out. Run. Hunt. Kill. Free.*

Not now, Trish told her desperately. *We're so close. This is our last chance. Please don't ruin it now.*

But there was no answer. She-Wolf never listened to her. It didn't matter if she asked or ordered, cajoled or yelled.

Or even if she begged.

Thunder rumbled again, and there was a flash of lightning in the distance. Trish quickened her pace on the dirt path, climbing uphill now.

To her left was a dark forest, tree branches swaying, the noise of the leaves like a sinister whisper.

To her right were open fields. The smell of prey seemed to engulf her from all directions. Deer. Rabbits. Sheep. Lots of sheep.

Silly, slow, bite-able sheep. Kill. Drink blood.

She could feel the nightmare rising up inside her—the churning, murderous, bloodthirsty darkness that was She-Wolf.

Where the hell was Tristan? The white wolf of the Silverlake pack, her best friend and protector. The only person she'd ever trusted with her shameful secret.

She needed him now. He'd have her medicine, to keep She-Wolf from going out of control.

NO! OUT NOW! She-Wolf snarled.

Trish fought her, wishing like hell that She-Wolf would listen to her just once. All they had to do was hang on a little longer, until they got their medicine. Until she got a chance to talk to Emon, the Draken Prince of Al-Maddeiri, the master of this territory.

The only one who might have the power to save them—if she just had enough time to win him over.

The path curved around a bend, and suddenly Al-Maddeiri's castle was looming over her in the darkness. A huge hulking shadow, looking as if it were crouching, waiting to attack. Even the yellow lights in a few of the windows didn't make it look homey or welcoming. They looked lonely and isolated, reminding her of primitive people huddled in caves, trying desperately to keep the darkness at bay with the tiny lights of their fires.

A sheet of lightning lit up the sky, so bright she saw purple afterimages. The thunder rumbled again—louder, closer.

Out! Run! Kill!

Darkness and churning rage swept through her.

Trish took a deep breath, gritting her teeth. She

fought the darkness away.

"This is what I get for reading so many damn fucking gothic romances," she muttered. "I'm sentenced to live in one."

Mysterious, lonely castle in the middle of nowhere: Check.

In fact, this was about as nowhere as it was possible to be—an interdimensional bubble between Earth and the Dragonlands. It was maybe the size of one of those tiny countries in Europe—Luxembourg or Lichtenstein. And outside its borders—literally nothing. An interdimensional void. The only way to get here was by a magical portal.

Dark and stormy night: Check.

Idiot heroine approaching the castle all alone, on the aforementioned dark and stormy night: Check.

No luggage, even—that had been sent over a week ago with the other healers and the research team. Who had probably all mysteriously disappeared by now, walled up in a dungeon or flamed into oblivion by…

The dark, dangerous, brooding master of the castle: Check.

Who lived here all alone with his mentally ill sister—and a few staff, presumably to cook entire oxen in a giant fireplace and throw Flintstone-sized pieces of it onto golden platters for him to devour.

Emon Lael, Darkwing Dragon, Prince of the Draken House of Al-Maddeiri. Rumor had it that he was unstable bordering on homicidal, his dragon too dangerous to be allowed into any civilized world. Even if he wanted to go to one, which rumor said he didn't. Apparently, he was planning on staying in this little bubble between the worlds, honing his brooding skills and thinking evil murdery dragon thoughts while snuggling his treasure hoard and slowly descending into insanity.

She just prayed that by some miracle, he could rescue her before that happened.

Another bolt of lightning forked through the sky, throwing monstrous shadows on the ground.

There was a huge 'crack' of thunder right overhead, hurting Trish's sensitive wolf ears and making her flinch. It was followed by a spectacular ripping sound, as multiple bolts of lightning split the dark clouds over the castle.

And into the lightning flew a huge black dragon, darker than the night sky, darker than a nightmare. Lightning forked down into his path, and instead of dodging it he flew right into it.

Trish gasped as a streak of lightning hit the dragon right between his wings. She expected him to fall from the sky, but instead, his whole body lit up, outlined by blue flames, scales reflecting blue and purple highlights as he rose into the storm. He gave a great roar of defiance, battling the wind currents, and then breathed twin lightning bolts from his nostrils as if trying to outdo the storm.

It struck again, and he was bathed in lightning once more, dipping and weaving, searching out the deadly bolts and drawing them to him.

He was wild, terrifying—and absolutely beautiful.

Trish stood, awestruck, watching the dragon dancing with the lightning. Once again She-Wolf rose within her, dark and wild.

Not now, she begged the wolf frantically. *Don't Change!*

She braced herself, waiting for the darkness to claw its way out of her. But She-Wolf went still: poised, waiting, staring up at the dragon until he abandoned the dance and disappeared into the darkness, and even after that.

Watching the sky, hoping he would return.

The wind was roaring around Trish now, whipping her long blond hair around her face. The rain would come soon.

She began walking again, faster, striding up the path to the main castle gates—huge, dragon-sized stone doors reinforced with iron and magic. They were closed, but a small human-sized door set into one of them was ajar. Trish pushed it open and walked inside, emerging into an immense stone courtyard.

The wind blustered and eddied, caught inside the stone walls. On the far side of the courtyard was a flight of wide, shallow steps leading up to the arched front door, also bound in iron. On either side was a lit sconce—the only light except for a few more lit windows dotted here and there above her.

For a real gothic touch, the sconces should have been flickering torches, but they were globes about the size of her head, giving a steady yellowish light. Not electric, or gas. Magical?

Trish took two steps into the courtyard and stopped, the back of her neck prickling with a hunter's instinct. She was being watched.

Everything in her screamed to stay in the shadows, but she had to get inside. Find Tristan. Calm her wolf, who was getting riled again. She heard herself growl, low in her throat.

"Okay, okay, I'm going," she murmured.

She forced herself to stride across the courtyard. Don't run. Predators attack if you run.

She was halfway across when the wind came howling down, bringing another crack of thunder, right overhead. A huge shadow descended out of the night, with a rush of wind and a scent of fire.

The dragon swooped down nearly on top of her, so close she could see its scales shining faintly in the glow of the lamplight. Its deadly black claw reached toward her. Then, with a great flap of its wings that sent grit and bits of debris swirling around her, it banked steeply upward, just missing the top of the wall on the far side.

It bugled, and fire erupted out of its mouth, a column of light in the sky.

The rain swept down.

Trish ran for the door, just ahead of a deluge of cold water. She stumbled up the worn stone steps and ducked under the overhang as the rain beat down behind her. Grasping the huge iron door-knocker in the shape of a dragon's head, she pounded it on the door, listening to the hollow boom as it echoed through the darkened castle.

CHAPTER 2

Emon Lael, Prince of the dead Draken House of Al-Maddeiri, flew high in the night, wrestling the storm.

Lightning bolts bathed him in electricity, setting his nerves tingling and his blood fizzing with life. He felt himself charging up like a battery, stoking the lightning that lived inside him.

He danced with the wind, twisting and shifting with the wild gusts and unpredictable currents. It was the only thing that made him feel fucking alive, anymore.

The only thing that kept his soul from solidifying into stone.

Pain lanced through him from the wound in his side—the one that was stealing his magic, the one that would never heal. The one that would one day eat him hollow, devouring his scales, his muscles, his organs, and finally his inner fire.

A slow, agonizing death sentence.

The only thing in his life still worth doing was helping his sister. Once Mayah was healed, she could leave this cursed place. Go to Earth, maybe. Find a mate among the Wild Dragons there. Or even maybe another kind of shifter, like his sister Kira had. Or Ashley Silver, the princess of the Akkabi clan, who'd mated a wolf.

Emon couldn't be saved. But maybe she could.

As he wheeled through the sky, something below caught his eye. Something—someone—moving in the courtyard of his castle.

Shining like a beacon in his magical sight—a bright star with a dark, mysterious core.

He stopped, hovering at the top of an updraft.

The earthbound star called to him.

She.

She called to him.

He beat his wings, banked sharply, and rode the currents down. As he reached her, his dragon suddenly took over control, extending his front leg with its sharp, deadly claws.

NO!

Emon exerted all his will, pulling up at the last second. He saw her upturned face, gazing at him in fear and awe, before she ran for what she thought was safety. Straight into his lair.

Little did she know, she would never be safe again.

He landed on the roof of the castle and stood in the torrential rain, resting his hands on the stone balustrade and staring down at the stranger standing at the great doors of his castle, pounding to be let inside.

<*Not a stranger*> said his dragon. <*We know her.*>

No, he thought slowly, not a stranger, though he'd never seen her before. Lithe, with long blond hair, tangled by in the wind.

And a nightmare inside.

<The Nightmare Wolf.>

His dragon had recognized her right away. It was why he'd done that crazy-ass dive into the courtyard, forcing Emon to nearly take out the top floor of the north wing on their way back up.

Emon gave a twisted grin. That would have severely inconvenienced the research team from the Silverlake wolf pack working up there. Especially because it probably would have killed most of them.

He wished he felt more upset about that thought, but he was numb. Numb with blocking everything out, with trying not to feel any of it: The loss of his clan; the years of captivity; the never-ending pain of his wound; the worry for his sister.

The fear of not managing to die before he was left totally alone.

<We need no one> his dragon said loftily.

He wished.

The words of the prophecy came back to him.

The Nightmare Wolf
Brings the end
Of all that came before.
Destruction.
Freedom.
Enemies devour you from within,
But she will break you, and the Darkwing Dragon will be
no more.

<Nonsense> said his dragon. <*She is only a wolf, like the others. No bigger than an appetizer. No mere wolf can destroy us.*>

Emon looked down again at the woman on his doorstep. His dragon saw a nightmare. He saw a shining star, a bright beacon.

He didn't know how both those things could exist in one woman, but he wanted to find out.

…destruction…freedom…

…she will break you, and the Darkwing Dragon will be no more.

Suddenly, he was almost looking forward to it.

CHAPTER 3

Trish stood at the huge door, the storm raging behind her, the back of her neck prickling. She felt like any second the dragon was going to swoop down and snatch her from the doorstep.

And what? Carry her off to his secret underground lair?

Rip her head off and crunch it like an M&M?

She-Wolf was still poised, waiting. For death? Or for a kindred spirit?

A dark, murdery kindred spirit.

Trish shivered.

Finally she heard footsteps inside, and then the huge castle door began to open. Trish braced herself, waiting for Frankenstein or a vampire or a creepy silent black-suited butler to appear.

What she got was a big, bulky man with a mane of wild blond hair, hazel eyes, and a friendly, quizzical expression. He wore khakis and a button-down shirt with the sleeves rolled up, and he was barefoot. He smelled like a lion.

For a second he stared at her, looking perplexed. Then his face cleared. "Ms. Waverly, right? The healer?"

"That's me," she said. "You can call me Trish."

"Come on in out of the rain." He held the door open, peering past her shoulder as if he, too, felt something behind her.

She stepped in and he closed the door, shutting out the storm. The sudden hush was almost startling.

"Sorry no one was at the portal to meet you," he said. "I didn't realize you were coming today."

That was weird. "I sent word to Tristan with the last supply shipment," she said. "And I got a note back from him."

"It might have slipped his mind. There was—an incident."

An *incident?* Like, a medical emergency? Or a dragon eating someone? Surely nothing had happened to Tristan, or he'd say so.

Before she could ask, he added, "I'm sorry. I'm Grange, the prince's Head Steward. Which in real-people language means I do All The Things, as far as running the castle and making sure everyone has what they need. So if you need anything, I'm your go-to guy."

Of course. No one went to the Darkwing Dragon for petty day-to-day things. When did royalty ever get their hands dirty? And by all accounts, Prince Emon was not exactly approachable.

Too bad that the things she needed, Grange couldn't give her. And she was beginning to doubt the dragon could either, if that near-death experience in the courtyard was anything to go by.

Don't give up hope yet, she told herself, trying to be

positive.

Right.

"Let me take your bag," Grange was saying politely. "I'll show you to your room."

"I can carry it," Trish said. She'd just carried it up the hill from the portal. It seemed stupid not to carry it the rest of the way.

Grange gave an apologetic half-smile. "Will it help if I tell you it's part of my job? Guests aren't supposed to carry their own luggage."

With a small sigh, Trish handed it over.

"Thank you," he said, his eyes crinkling with humor. "You just saved me from being thrown in the dungeon for dereliction of duty."

"There's not really a dungeon here, is there?" Trish asked. Please, let there be a dungeon. Because that would be *so* cool.

"Oh, yeah," Grange said. "If you're good, I'll take you to see it sometime."

"Now there's something to look forward to," Trish said. He grinned.

Grange led her out of the entranceway—annnnnd, they were back in the gothic novel again. They'd stepped into a Great Hall straight out of some medieval castle on Earth. Enormous, with tall arched windows and a vaulted ceiling, and staircases winding up both side walls. There was a huge fireplace, unlit, and the room was chilly and bleak and cheerless.

Perfect.

Except for Grange, who was as friendly-looking as a

puppy, and had a kind of golden glow like the sun was constantly shining on him. Not to mention how dorky he looked with her bag over his shoulder, the size of a child's purse compared to his huge bulk.

Definitely not fitting in with the gothic vibe. She gave a little laugh.

"What?" Grange asked, running his hand over his wild hair and looking concerned. "I'm a mess, right? Or do I have a piece of broccoli stuck in my fangs?"

Trish shook her head. "Sorry," she said. "You're just ...not what I expected."

"What were you expecting?" he asked, sounding curious rather than offended. He started for one of the staircases, and she fell into step with him.

"Oh, you know. A hatchet-faced housekeeper, muttering curses under her breath. Or a timid maid who hints at dark goings-on in the dead of night."

"Ah," he said. "How about a ghost complete with rattling chains, or an enigmatic butler—tightlipped and disapproving?" He grinned at her look of surprise. "I saw your books when the maid unpacked your stuff. My mom reads them too. Sadly, I'm just an ordinary lion shifter. The best I can do is mutter dark warnings about evil ghosts."

"That would be awesome," Trish said. "It would be even better if there are some. Please tell me there are."

He snorted. "If there aren't, there should be. This place was made for them." As they climbed the stairs, he added, "I still feel bad there was no one to meet you. You really shouldn't have been out there alone."

He was right—she shouldn't. She-Wolf had almost taken over, which would have been a disaster. Ironically, if it hadn't been for the dragon and her fascination with it, she probably would have.

But he didn't know about that. Couldn't be allowed to know about that. "I'm a wolf," she said lightly. "I can handle a half-mile walk and a little weather."

"It's not that." He stopped, lowering his voice. "It's the Darkwing Dragon," he said quietly. "He goes a little crazy when it storms." He turned and started up the stairs, but she heard him mutter, "Crazier than usual."

Awesome. "He's not…dangerous, is he?"

Okay, that was stupid. He breathed lightning and he was halfway insane, not to mention pissed-off all the time. Of course he was dangerous. She qualified. "Like, eating people dangerous?"

She expected Grange to laugh, but he just shrugged again. Double awesomeness.

"All Draken are dangerous," he said, "and the House of Al-Maddeiri were always the most dangerous. And these two—the prince and princess—well, you know what happened to them. That's why you're here."

CHAPTER 4

Everybody in the Silverlake wolf pack knew what had happened to the prince and princess of the House of Al-Maddeiri.

Captured as children and raised by an evil wizard after their clan was wiped out, only to be used as lab rats in his experiments. Emon had been his guinea pig for some kind of toxin that would specifically affect Draken—which were powerful, magical, and almost impossible to kill.

It had left him cursed with a near-fatal wound that would never heal.

With Mayah, the princess, the wizard Ragnor had drugged her and made her push the boundaries of the Al-Maddeiri mental powers, leaving her with nightmares, visions and hallucinations.

Their sister Kira, mate to Flynn, alpha of the Bad Blood Crew, had found them after over twenty years had passed. The Silverlake pack had backed up her and Flynn and the rest of the Bad Bloods on the rescue mission, fighting a huge battle in the valley just below the castle, killing Ragnor and his hellhounds.

Now, after over a year, Emon had finally agreed to

let a carefully vetted group of shifter scientists have access to Ragnor's research—in return for Silverlake's top team of mental healers coming here for an indefinite period of time, to try to help Mayah recover.

Which was what Tristan was doing here. As a white wolf, he had mental powers of his own, including the ability to get inside the minds of damaged shifters and help them heal.

Trish was here only because Tristan had somehow persuaded Mina Reilly, head of the research group, that she would be a valuable addition to the team. No one else knew her real purpose.

Trish said now, "You said there was some kind of incident? Is everyone all right?"

Grange hunched his big shoulders uncomfortably. "More or less. The princess had one of her really bad days, that's all. Crazy visions, nightmare hallucinations..."

That didn't sound good. "I thought the treatment was going well," Trish said. At least, Tristan had thought so, last she'd heard. "What happened?"

Grange looked straight ahead. "I really shouldn't say. It's better if you get a report from the team."

He'd led her up the stairs and down a couple of corridors, and now they were headed up another staircase. Trish was losing track of where she was; this place was like a maze. She could feel She-Wolf scrabbling at her insides again. She did *not* like it in here.

Don't Change. Please don't Change.

All the hallways seemed dim, though they were lit

with the same kind of light globes she'd seen on the outside of the door. It was more the atmosphere—bleak bare stone, no carpets, the echoes from their footsteps sounding eerie and desolate.

And lonely.

Once or twice Trish caught a glimpse of someone far down a hall or crossing the end of a corridor—staff, probably. Other than that, she and Grange might have been alone in this place.

How did Emon and Mayah stand it?

Maybe they didn't. He'd said they were crazy. Trish got that—if she didn't see her people soon, she might be headed for crazytown herself.

She-Wolf pushed at her. *Out. Out. Bad place.*

Not yet, Trish begged. *We're almost there.* Hopefully.

Grange led her up a couple of stairs, then down a few more, around corners, and into a long hallway. "Here we are," he said. "The research team is on a different floor, but Mr. Barnes requested that you be placed near him and the Reillys. There's a salon at the end, where you can all relax, and a couple more common rooms upstairs in the research wing."

He opened a doorway and ushered her into her room, turning on one of the light globes.

Whoa.

It was at least four times the size of a normal bedroom, its high ceiling making it feel like a cavern. Canopied bed with purple velvet curtains, matching drapes on the mullioned windows. Thick carpets that looked hand-woven; velvet and brocade upholstered couches and chairs made out of heavy dark wood; tapestries on the stone walls depicting Draken in battle—lots of blood, fire, dead bodies, and gaping wounds.

Nice. Very soothing.

The room was dim and cold, and Grange went around turning on the lights, showing her how the light globes worked by touching their metal base. He put her bag down on a carved wooden chest at the foot of the bed and grinned at her.

"So, what do you think? Gothic enough for you?"

"More than I could ever ask for," she said truthfully.

"Like I said, one of the maids already unpacked for you and put your things away. The bathroom is through there." He gestured at a door across the room. "If you need anything, there's a bell rope right here." He touched a long strip of velvet embroidered with flames, attached to the wall.

"A bell rope? Are you serious? Does it ring in a dim squalid basement servants' hall?" Trish went over to touch it. "This is really some kind of gothic novel sub-dimension, isn't it?"

Grange grinned, glancing over to where the books Trish had sent ahead in her luggage were stacked on a side table.

"Damn, you figured it out. I guess I might as well go ahead and tell you that I'm the secret half brother of the royal family, just waiting to bump them off so I can inherit everything." He tried to grin evilly, which totally didn't work on him, and added. "I can have a mute servant with a mysterious scar come in and light the fire, if you want."

"I'd take you up on that if I thought you really meant it, but you're just toying with me, aren't you."

He grinned for real and shrugged. "Not about the fire."

"I think I'm okay for now."

"Okay then. I'll leave you to get settled." He paused in the doorway, then added, "Welcome to the dark and gloomy House of Al-Maddeiri, in exile."

He left, breaking into an Oscar-worthy evil villain laugh that echoed down the hall as he walked away.

She kind of liked that guy.

Too bad he wasn't the one she needed help from.

Trish pressed the heels of her hands to her temples. She'd been joking to keep She-Wolf at bay, but now the wolf was tearing at her insides again. *Out! Out!*

You can't come out! But her wolf was in a mood, and when she was in a mood she was uncontrollable. Maybe some fresh air would help, until Trish could find Tristan.

She went over to the window. It was a casement style that opened like double doors, and she pushed open one side and leaned out.

The air was chilly and it was still raining, though the thunder and lightning had passed overhead. Trish breathed deeply and tried to calm her wolf down.

She scanned the sky, looking for the Darkwing Dragon, but there was nothing above but windswept skies.

Then, slowly, a great shadowy shape rose from below her. A huge head appeared, not three feet in front of her, its eyes glowing electric green.

Trish froze, looking straight into the dragon's eyes as it hovered outside her window, staring back at her.

No, not 'it'. Him. She knew in the marrow of her bones that this was Prince Emon.

His pupils were black slits, with lightning dancing in the center. His tongue snaked out between his giant pointed fangs, as if he were licking his chops.

Looking at a snack.

Good dragon, she thought, too frozen to speak. *No biting.*

He gave a little huff of air, almost as if he were laughing. Then his shoulder muscles bunched and the midnight black wings swooshed down, propelling him upwards.

In a moment, he was gone.

Trish backed up until she hit one of the chairs and sank into it, shaking.

She-Wolf was howling inside her, and Trish doubled over with a sudden cramp. Two of her ribs snapped, her body shimmering with the beginnings of the Change.

Fuck, fuck, fuck. She couldn't Change in this room—She-Wolf would destroy it, and everyone would know she was rogue. It was too high to jump from the window. Could she make it outside? But how would she explain?

As another cramp hit her, she saw a piece of folded paper on top of her stack of books. Her name was on the outside, in Tristan's slanted handwriting.

With a shaking hand, she reached out to grab it.

If you're reading this, I couldn't get away to meet you. I'll come find you as soon as I can. In the meantime, check this place out. It's like one of your books. And don't forget to look in the bathroom—it's amazing. Everything you could need is in there.

She dropped the note on the table. The bathroom. Everything she could need. Tris hadn't forgotten her after all.

She dashed for the door Grange had indicated, wobbling slightly on legs trying to turn wolf. Groping on the base of the wall sconce, she turned the light globe on. Her cosmetics and toiletries had been set out next to the marble sink, looking lonely on the vast countertop.

Below it was a set of small drawers. Inside the top one was a thin leather case containing two syringes.

Tristan, I love you, she thought fervently. *You're my very bestest friend.*

She closed the bathroom door and sat on the lid of the thronelike toilet, trying to still her trembling hand. She-Wolf was fighting her, but she managed to get the syringe into her vein and push the plunger.

She-Wolf howled furiously. Trish leaned back and closed her eyes, feeling tears gathering. The darkness receded, and her body settled back into human form.

As She-Wolf's voice faded, the tears spilled down Trish's cheeks. *I'm sorry,* she said to her wolf, not knowing if she could hear. *I'm so sorry...*

CHAPTER 5

It took about fifteen minutes for the drug to kick in. For Trish to feel normal.

If 'normal' meant she couldn't hear or feel her wolf.

She dashed the tears away from her cheeks and hid the syringe back in the drawer. That drug was experimental, and it was illegal for her to have any.

Tristan was taking a big risk, getting it for her. She owed him so big she could never repay him.

I need to convince Emon to help me, she told herself. *Somehow. I can't keep doing this to Tristan, letting him risk himself for me.*

So she had to figure out how to make friends with a dragon.

In the meantime, she had to pretend everything was all right. She got up and splashed cold water on her face.

Find something else to think about. Focus on the good stuff.

Like this kickass pseudo-Victorian Draken bathroom. She took a deep breath looked around, finally able to take in its spectacular awesomeness. It was bigger than her bedroom back at Silverlake, and had a huge marble shower with enough room for a party, with shiny brass pipes and nozzles and faucets. Very steampunk.

Also, a giant-sized bathtub almost big enough to swim in, with a surround of some dark polished wood. The toilet was also crazy old-fashioned, with the water tank attached to the wall overhead, and a pull-chain to flush it.

Trish pulled on the chain experimentally, and the water rushed loudly down a brass pipe into the toilet, sounding like Niagara Falls in the spring.

Sweet. And another up side—she wasn't going to have to poop in a hole with a four-story drop underneath it, like some European medieval castles she'd seen on the History Channel. Anything could crawl up inside a toilet like that. Snakes. Tarantulas. The Loch Ness monster's interdimensional cousin. Poop squids with slimy tentacles.

She patted the throne-toilet in gratitude. *Positive thoughts.*

Continuing on the up side, there were lots of fluffy towels, and something that even looked like a towel warmer, if she could figure out how to turn it on without dragon magic.

Okay. She was calmer now. Next project—find Tristan and the research team. It was mid-afternoon back at Silverlake, but she had no clue what time it was here. Were they working? Sleeping? Eating dinner?

And where did dinner happen, anyway? Grange had said nothing about food.

Should she pull the bell rope and ask whoever came

to point her to the research team and the dining area? But would that mean some poor maid would have to schlepp all the way from the basement up to here, just to answer a question?

That seemed wrong.

Maybe she could find them on her own.

She opened the door to the bedroom, and immediately was hit with a sense of wrongness. Her hackles rose in warning. Something was off.

The window was closed.

Had she done that? She didn't think so. Maybe it had blown shut?

She walked slowly over to it. It wasn't just closed, it was latched.

Behind her, she heard the fireplace ignite with a soft *whump.* A voice said, "Interesting books. What's with all the women running through the woods in their nightgowns?"

Trish jumped about a mile and a half, and whirled around to see a man leaning his hips against the edge of the table, dressed in black leather and looking like a piece of midnight come to life. With a bunch of her books in his hands.

Where no one had been standing a minute ago.

It could only be one person.

"You're Emon," she croaked, her throat dry from the sudden shock. "The Darkwing Dragon."

Holy fuck. Him. Here. Now.

She had not even heard him come in. Or scented him. How the fuck could that happen?

He shouldn't be here yet. She was totally unprepared. To make him like her. Or deal with his immense presence. It filled the room, pressing on her chest, like an alpha wolf on steroids.

"I saw you," she said inanely. "Outside my window."

Duh.

He raised his eyes to her. His were glittering green, hard and bright like emeralds.

"I was curious about you."

Curious enough to break into her room like a sexy stealth ninja, apparently. She wasn't sure that was a good thing. No. Probably not. Although at least he couldn't eat her in this form. Well, not in the bad bitey death kind of way. Only in the sex kind of way. Heat rushed to her core.

Oh, shit. Stop thinking that.

"And I saw you in the courtyard," she went on, queen of the obvious, her mouth continuing to move on its own with no input from her brain. Probably because all the blood had rushed south, between her legs. "I thought for a second there you were going to carry me off to your lair."

He didn't deny it. "Technically, this whole place is my lair," he said. He gazed at her, his look predatory and assessing, the rest of him sexy as sin. "Unless you mean the underground dungeon where I chain up the pretty maidens I kidnap, and do terrible, evil, perverted things to them."

Okay, he was messing with her now. Probably.

Although that didn't stop her lady parts from wanting to do something really stupid. And dammit, by the look on his face, he knew it.

He added, "Don't worry. My lair is soundproof. No one will hear you screaming." He waited a beat. "Or panting. Or howling." His gaze dropped to her boobs, and then her crotch, before returning to her face.

Definitely messing with her. Unfortunately for him, she'd grown up with Rafe Connors, the sexual innuendo champion of the entire western United States. Not only was she immune, she could embarrass the fuck out of him with one paw tied behind her back.

"FYI, wolves like it from behind," she said. "And I hope you're not the kind of guy who wants a blow job and then just rolls over and goes to sleep, without the girl getting even a teeny, weeny little orgasm. Because that's just rude."

Oh, shit. She wasn't supposed to be embarrassing him. She was supposed to be making him like her.

Luckily, her smartassiness seemed to amuse him instead—at least, his mouth twisted in what she thought was a smile. Kind of a.

"Is that an offer?" he asked.

No. Yes? Even without a smile, he was melt-your-panties *hot*. Big, muscled all over, with wavy black hair that still looked windswept and sexy, chiseled features, and those emerald eyes.

"Show me your sex dungeon, and we'll talk." No, no no no. *Yes*, her lady-parts said. *Definitely yes.*

He gave a snort of almost-laughter. She'd made him

laugh. At least it meant he wasn't feeling murdery. Probably.

"So is that what happens in these books?" He nodded at the gothic romances fanned out in his hands. Sexy hands. Large and strong.

"God, no," she said. "These are old-school. They have no sex at all in them."

He looked perplexed. "Then what's the point?"

Mental sigh. Men. The point was…wait, what was the point of no sex again? Oh, right.

"Romance," she said. "Passion, longing, soulmates…" He didn't look convinced. She sighed out loud. "There's more to life than your dick, you know."

Whoops. She put her hand over her mouth. You didn't talk to a prince about his dick. Especially when you just met him.

He just smirked. "Wait until you've been chained in my dungeon for awhile. You'll change your mind."

She rolled her eyes. "In your dreams."

That corner of his mouth was definitely headed in a smiley direction. Ha. The prince liked sassy wolves. He looked down at the books again. "Really? No sex at all?"

"No, perv." Keep the sassy going. "Except a few passionate kisses, when the dark, dangerous, enigmatic hero can't hold back his feelings anymore. But then he disappears into the gloomy castle for days, brooding. Because he's no good for her."

"Uh huh. So if there's no sex, why are they all running around in their nightgowns?" He held up the books. He was not wrong; all the covers showed women running through dark forests in flowy white nightgowns. "Is it an Earth custom I don't know about?"

"Yes," Trish said, deadpan. "It's called 'marketing.'"

He raised his eyebrows, clearly not getting the joke. She sighed.

"These are all gothic romances, in which a woman goes to live in a big gloomy old house or castle for some stupid reason, falls in love with the dark and brooding master of the house, uncovers deep dark secrets, almost dies for some other stupid reason, and finally discovers he loves her too and lives happily ever after."

"Sounds fascinating," Emon said. "Not." But that kind-of smile was still hovering around his mouth. "Where does the nightgown come in?"

"It doesn't," Trish said. "They hardly ever run around outside in their nightgowns, but it's on all the covers anyway. Like a signal, so you know it's a gothic romance. Just like all those steamy romances have naked man-chest on the covers."

She really needed to get him off this topic. Because now she was picturing his naked man-chest. "You know it's not socially acceptable to carry women you just met off to your sex dungeon, right?" she said. "They told you that in prince school?"

"I was raised by an evil wizard," he said. "So no. My conversational skills suck. The Bad Bloods have been trying to educate me, but..." He spread his arms in a gesture of futility. "Clearly the lessons haven't stuck."

Trish snorted. "Seriously? You're expecting to learn manners from the Bad Blood Crew? That's like trying to get an earthworm to teach you how to fly."

"Lucky for me, I already know how to fly." Yep, that mouth-thing was definitely a smile.

"Okay, well, just because the no-sex-until-after-mating thing is outdated for most shifters, doesn't mean they all want to come to your sex dungeon. And some people are waiting for their true mate to come along."

He ran his finger down the stack of books. "So you're waiting for The One?"

For some reason, the question hit Trish like a knife straight to the heart.

The One.

A fated mate, bonded for life with utter devotion. Like Jace and Emma, her pack leaders. Or Kane, their Enforcer, and his mate Rachelle. Or Mina, head of the research team, and her mate Noah, who were here with their son Brock.

Something she, with her broken wolf, would never have.

She shrugged one shoulder. "They're just books. Don't read too much into it."

He gave a brief nod of acknowledgement, but his eyes were still on her. Thinking. Assessing. Searching deep inside her, where the darkness was waiting.

She felt suddenly exposed, like he could rip her chest open and lay all her secrets bare, leaving her to bleed.

Hell, he was an Al-Maddeiri Draken, with mind powers. He probably could.

She shivered, despite the warmth of the fire.

He narrowed his eyes. "So why are you here, Trish Waverly?" He knew her name? "Besides a dark desire to be chained up in my sex dungeon?"

He'd figured out she had an agenda. But this wasn't the time to blurt out all her troubles and beg him for help. She had to wait until her brain was fully functioning, and she could figure out the best way to bring it up.

"I—I'm just part of the research team."

He stared into her eyes, and she felt like a rabbit in a hawk's sights, frozen in fear, knowing her doom was coming but unable to get out of the way.

"Come to dinner tonight," he said suddenly.

What?

"The formal dining room. Drinks in the drawing room first. One hour. Don't be late, it pisses off the chef."

"Um, okay? Will anyone else—"

He didn't even let her finish. With terrifying suddenness he was right there, looming over her, one hand wrapped around her neck. She'd barely seen him move.

He lowered his head and kissed her, his lips hot and hard on hers. She froze for a second, and then heat flooded through her and her lips parted on their own. His softened against hers, deepening the kiss, his tongue meeting hers in a silken dance.

After an eternity, he pulled away. His pupils had elongated into vertical black slits with lightning in their depths. Oh, hell. Dragon.

His hand tightened around her throat, and when he spoke, his voice was low, raspy, and completely terrifying.

"Stay away from him, Nightmare Wolf," it said. "You are right. He is no good for you."

Trish felt her eyes go round and wide. Holy fuck.

Another one of those lightning moves, and he was at the door. He turned back to her, his dragon still in his eyes, and in his voice. "And you will not destroy me."

He was out the door and gone before she even had a chance to open her mouth.

CHAPTER 6

Emon leaned against the wall outside the door to Trish's room. His heart was racing, his dick was throbbing, and his brain seemed to have completely shut down.

She was a witch. Had to be.

One minute he'd been inviting the fucking Nightmare Wolf to dinner—why?—and the next he was outside her door, without knowing how he got there.

Did something just happen? he asked his dragon. Then another suspicion crossed his mind. *Did you do something?*

Silence.

You did, didn't you?

<*I have no idea what you're talking about.*>

Oh, fuck. His dragon was running amok, his magic was barely working, *and* he'd invited the Nightmare Destructo-Wolf to dinner. Why the hell had he even done that?

Because she was beautiful. Not just on the outside. She was a shining star inside, just like he'd seen from the sky. Warm and bright. Just being near her made him feel…things.

He didn't feel things. Not anymore.

But she made that cold ball of ice in the center of his chest feel like it was melting. Just a little.

It had made him want to spend more time with her. Which bad for everyone. Numb was better. He hardly ever wanted to kill people when he was numb.

It had also made him for real want to drag her off and take her from behind, bury himself in her and make her howl with pleasure. He wondered how long it would actually take to set up a sex dungeon.

<*I'm sure you could adapt one of the actual dungeons.*>
Thanks for the tip.

Damn women all to hell. No good could come of this.

He'd only gone to her room to meet her, get a feel for how dangerous she was.

The answer: more dangerous than he could possibly have imagined.

All that silky blond hair that begged him to slide his fingers through it, wrap it in his fist and pull her head back to kiss the pulsing vein in her throat.

Cornflower-blue eyes filled with sassy perverted humor and…a deep-down goodness. Caring.

And a love of romantic Earth books about dark brooding men in lonely castles. True love. And happily ever after.

All wrapped around that tantalizing darkness inside. The killer. The wolf.

His dragon didn't know what to make of her.

Neither did he.

But he knew he was going to browbeat the chef into

whipping up a formal dinner in under an hour.

And he'd better send someone to tell Tristan Barnes and the Reillys that they were expected for dinner too. More people, to keep him from doing something really crazy, like shoving the dinner on the floor and getting Trish naked on the huge dining table.

Fuck. Stop thinking about that.

Maybe he should invite Mayah too. He wouldn't lose control if she were there. Probably. Hopefully.

He hoped she'd be well enough to come. He wished he knew what was causing these episodes. She'd seem to be getting better, and then for no reason she'd have a total meltdown, complete with hallucinations.

Her dragon had receded deep inside her—she didn't even Change anymore. They were both wasting away—him from his physical wound, and her from her mental ones.

He had to save her. All these years, since he was three years old, he'd protected his little sister. It was the only accomplishment he had to be proud of in his whole damn life.

If she slipped away into the darkness, his entire existence would have been worth nothing.

He went upstairs to his study and pulled out his in-house communicator, a round golden ball about two inches in diameter, powered by magic.

He called the kitchen and put in his dinner order, cutting off the chef when the sputtering, complaining, and cries of "But this is impossible" got too boring.

Then he sat down in his desk chair with a sigh, running his hand through his hair.

He was still buzzing from the storm lightning. It charged him up, gave him back some of the energy the wound was sapping from him. It was a temporary fix, but it should last for a few days, maybe a week.

Hell, he should get Silverlake to send him one of the generators they were using to power their research equipment, and just hook himself up to that.

Graft some scales from a river *raka* onto his wound, and turn himself into FrankenDragon, like that movie he'd watched with Flynn and Kira and Xander.

If only that would work.

There was a hollow, musical sound, and the larger communicator on his desk lit up. He sighed and plucked the ball out of his stand.

"Al-Maddeiri here," he said. "Whatever the fuck you want, can't it wait until tomorrow?"

A disgruntled voice came back. "Oh, am I disturbing your exalted Highness? So sorry I didn't have time to call during business hours. I was busy slaving away in your mine, adding to your great wealth and earning my own pittance."

Emon rolled his eyes. "Zakerek," he said. "What do you need to whine about today?"

Zakerek and his two cohorts were Wild Dragons who had once worked for Ragnor, the evil fucking wizard who'd held Emon and Mayah prisoner here for decades.

The red dragon's face appeared on the surface of the

communicator. "Me?" he said. "I'm not the one who left a message whinging about losing a couple of mangy sheep, and accusing us of taking them."

"It wasn't a couple of sheep," Emon said. "It was nineteen. Two were pregnant ewes, and several were slated for shearing."

"Whatever," Zakerek said. "We still didn't do it, being ever so happy to subsist on the scraps you so graciously give us." Sarcasm dripped from his voice.

Emon growled. "Don't piss me off, Wild Dragon. Just because I didn't kill you after the battle, doesn't mean I can't do it now."

He'd had every right to kill all three of them—they'd colluded with the man who'd kidnapped and tortured the royal line of Al-Maddeiri. This outpost was all that was left of Al-Maddeiri territory, and the old laws still held here.

Or whatever laws were enacted by the Ruling Council. Which was basically him.

But he'd had enough of killing and death, and in a moment of soft-heartedness he'd paroled them instead, sentencing them to mining *atherias*—the rare and magical mineral that financed his entire domain.

"Sure, kill us," Zakerek said. "If you want to mine your own damn *atherias*, which you don't. You're as stuck with us as we are with you. You do have a wolf pack living in your castle, by the way. Wolves? Sheep? Duh. So maybe go talk to them about your little complaint, and leave us alone. Zakerek out."

He disconnected before Emon could ask him about

this month's yield. His reports were late—again—and Emon needed to know if they were going to earn enough to build the bridge and aqueduct needed over by the western farms.

He was going to have to fly out to the mine in the next few days, which he was not looking forward to. Zakerek always gave him a headache.

He couldn't tell if Zakerek was telling the truth about the sheep. He couldn't imagine who else would have taken them—he doubted very much that the research team had hunted and killed nineteen sheep and made them disappear without a trace.

On the other hand, Zakerek would enjoy pissing Emon off by stealing sheep. And if he and the other dragons were running short of game to hunt, he'd be too proud to ask Emon for food.

He should check whether there were enough dragon-sized munchies in the forest near the mine. As much as the Wild Dragons annoyed him, he didn't want them to starve.

He wasn't a complete monster.

Only about eighty percent.

He leaned back in his chair, rubbing his eyes with his thumb and middle finger. He didn't need this shit. Not today.

Not with his potential destruction coming to dinner.

CHAPTER 7

After Emon left the room, Trish sank down in the nearest chair, every hair on her body standing on end.

What the actual fuck had just happened there?

Emon's dragon had *talked* to her. Just taken over his body and did it. She'd never heard of someone's animal doing that.

She didn't even think he realized what had happened. That right there was exorcist horror-movie shit.

And now she was supposed to figure out how to dress for an impromptu formal dinner with the 'dark, dangerous, brooding master of the house', who could start randomly talking to her like a demon-possessed monster at any time. In between toe-curling kisses.

If she didn't still need his help, she would totally be skipping dinner.

Of course, if this were one of her books, she would have the perfect ravishing gown in her trunk—one that would make him instantly fall in love with her.

But she had no trunk, no gowns, and no weapons in her arsenal of feminine wiles capable of turning a demon-possessed monster into a puddle of devoted moosh.

She was fucked.

Should she try to look slutty and alluring instead? She didn't actually need to make him fall in love with her—all she needed was to soften him up enough so that he might consider using his Al-Maddeiri superpowers to help her control her wolf.

On the other hand, this whole scenario was quickly sliding downhill from gothic romance into horror movie territory. And everyone knew who the first victim was in the horror movie. The slutty blonde.

She finally went with something less victim-y: black skinny pants, a sparkly black top, and one of her favorite pairs of glitter sneakers.

Glitter sneakers were Trish's other guilty pleasure. She picked out her dressiest pair—wedge sneakers with gold and silver glitter—and put them on. After taking extra care with her makeup, she headed for the dining room, giving herself plenty of time.

She thought.

Problem one: She had no fucking clue where the dining room was.

Problem two: Once she'd been down a few corridors and made a few turns, she had no clue how to get back to her room either.

She finally found a random staircase and was heading downward when she heard a hollow moaning sound.

She froze. That didn't sound like the wind. It sounded like...

No. No ghosts. This was not a gothic subdimension. Or a horror movie.

The sound came again, and then came a murmuring, whispering sound, like the ghosts were having a conversation.

The hair stood up on the back of her neck.

Instead of going down, Trish crept up the stairs, toward the source of the sound.

Because that's what horror movie victims always did. Went *toward* the bad shit instead of away from it. She might as well have gone ahead and put on the slutwear.

She paused on the upper landing. The whispering was a bit louder here, but still faint. It sounded like it was coming from a curtained alcove about twenty feet down the hall.

Trish crept softly toward the alcove. Maybe it was just two servants talking, but her hackles were still standing up. Just as she reached the alcove, everything went silent.

She hesitated. She couldn't scent anyone inside. Did she really want to pull the curtains back and see a bloody decapitated ghost? Talking?

Fuck it.

She swept the velvet curtains back in a sharp, sudden movement.

There was no one inside the alcove—just a window with a cushioned window seat.

Trish stood still, listening, but the noise had definitely stopped. She felt a presence, though—as if something was in the alcove, watching her.

So. Creepy.

Slowly, Trish backed out of the alcove and let the curtain drop. She turned and headed back down the hall, walking faster and faster. She went down the staircase at a run and stopped at the bottom, panting.

The sense of a presence was gone.

By the time she found a maid and got directions to the dining room, she was almost ready to laugh at herself. All this spooky atmosphere was getting to her. There sure as shit hadn't been ghosts having a conference in the alcove.

Probably.

Finally Trish found the dining room. It was empty of people, the long polished table formally set for seven, with crystal, china and two elaborate silver candelabra in the center, still unlit.

The drawing room should be across the hall.

It, too, was empty, though there was a log fire burning in the fireplace, and the lamp globes were lit. It was furnished in the same ornate style as her bedroom: dark wood furniture, velvet and brocade, and way too many knickknacks and figurines made of gold and porcelain and a purplish metallic substance she didn't recognize. Everything looked heavy, expensive, and rarely used.

Unless Emon was one of those psychos who replaced everything as soon as it got a little tear or stain or worn spot. She'd read a truly terrifying book about a guy like that.

There was a tray with decanters set up on the

sideboard, but Trish didn't feel comfortable just pouring herself a drink, especially since she didn't know what was in any of the decanters.

She'd assumed the places at the table were for some of the other researchers: Mina and Noah, probably, and Tristan—but if so, where were they?

She could almost believe they'd disappeared, and she was alone in the castle with two half-insane dragons.

Or maybe all the way insane.

Too antsy to sit, she wandered over to the fireplace and looked at the painting above it. Not Emon, as she half-expected.

Instead, it was a portrait of a handsome blond man in a black robe, with two dogs at his feet.

It was a decent enough painting, if you liked that sort of thing. It beat the blood-and-death tapestries in her bedroom.

But the more she looked at it, the more it disturbed her. The man's mouth had a cruel twist to it, and he looked way too damn pleased with himself. His too-pretty face was pocked with scars, like he'd had super-bad acne at some point.

She wondered why the artist had painted that in.

His hands were cupped, and in between them was a ball of black fire. And on closer inspection, she could see that the "dogs" at his feet had glowing orange eyes.

Hellhounds? Who the fuck would want to be painted with hellhounds, like they were pets?

Unless...

"Please tell me this isn't a painting of Ragnor," she

muttered.

"Yep," said a voice behind her, followed by the unmistakable whirring sound of a blade being thrown. Trish ducked, looking up just in time to watch an eight-inch knife bury itself point-first in Ragnor's left eye.

Thwak.

She turned to see Emon leaning against the wall, like he'd been there all along.

"Do you always have to sneak into a room like a ninja dragon?" she demanded. "What happened to just walking in the normal way?"

"What fun is that?"

He walked over to stand next to her. He, unlike her, had *not* dressed up—he was still wearing the dusty black leathers he'd had on in her room. Men. As he got closer she could feel the heat of his body, hotter than the fireplace. Fire and lightning, two of the most dangerous things in all the worlds, burning inside him, waiting to be ignited.

Note to self: Do not ignite the dragon. So maybe she shouldn't yell at him? Only, her brain seemed to quit working when she was around him.

He nodded up at the painting. "That's Ragnor, all right. The man who raised us, educated us, caged us, poisoned us, and made my sister and me into the people we are today."

Tortured. Damaged. Half-insane.

Trish looked closer at the painting. Those weren't acne scars on Ragnor's face. They were holes in the canvas.

"You keep his portrait to throw knives at?"

Emon shrugged. "Kira told me that putting his head on a pike in front of the castle and watching the crows pull his face off would be uncivilized."

Yikes. "Um, probably."

"So there you go." He turned to her. "Want to try? Bet you can't hit his right eye, little wolf."

Okay, now he'd made a mistake. "Challenge accepted, Draken Prince," she said. "Bring on the knives."

CHAPTER 8

She'd dressed up, Emon realized.

For some absurd reason, that pleased him. Especially because she was wearing black—his favorite color.

It looked a lot better on Trish than on him. It set off her hair and her skin, making them look luminescent and making him want to attack the pale column of her neck, leaving her with love bites to remember him by.

Her top was decorated with some shiny gold stuff in the shape of a starburst. As if she knew how she looked to him.

The pants hugged her curves, making her luscious, rounded ass look good enough to eat. In a non-dragony, completely sexual way.

Wolves like it from behind.

He could feel a boner popping up inside his own pants. He tried to erase the visual of watching that ass as he leaned her over the edge of the bed and drove into her from behind, but no. It was permanent.

To distract her from what was going on with his crotch, he said, "I like your shoes."

He did like them; they were shiny, like her top.

Covered in gold and silver sparkly glitter, and they had some kind of chunky heels on them that somehow made her legs look even hotter.

"Thanks," she said, turning her foot this way and that, catching the light. "I have some for every mood. Purple are my favorite, but you gotta match the outfit."

He wondered what the mood of this particular outfit was supposed to be. Sexy? Formal? Dragon-defying?

She added, "Glitter sneakers are my secret vice."

He said, "I thought gothic novels were your secret vice. And sex from behind while wearing chains. You're stacking up the vices, my wolfy friend."

"I have an endless supply of vices," she said, gazing up into his eyes with her cornflower-blue ones, a hint of a secret smile hovering on those tasty-as-fuck lips. "You have no idea."

There went the boner again.

He went to the sideboard and opened a drawer, pulling out three more knives, perfectly balanced for throwing. He held them out to her, hoping she wouldn't notice his erectile situation.

"I'll even give you three chances," he said.

"Such a gentleman," she murmured.

Not even a little bit.

She took the knives, weighing one in her hand, then grasped the tip and hefted it to feel the balance. "Nice," she said.

She backed up a bit to get a good line of fire at Ragnor, flexed her elbow a couple of times to line up her shot, and threw.

Thwak. Thwak. Thwak.

All perfect shots. Right eye. Throat. And...

Crotch.

Emon winced. "Was that last one really necessary?"

She shrugged. "Still more civilized than watching crows eat his face off."

Emon wasn't so sure about that.

You would have thought that seeing her impale Ragnor in the nuts would have taken the edge off his lust, but no. Apparently, watching a woman go all lethal and badass was a turn-on for him.

"I won the bet," she said, turning to him. "What do I get?"

He could think of about a dozen things he wanted to give her. One of them was currently about to burst out of his pants.

"How about a drink?"

"What have you got? The blood of your enemies, maybe?" She was teasing him. He loved the way it made her eyes dance and her mouth turn up at the corners.

"I'm out of that. I'm waiting for someone to piss me off so I can restock."

The smile deepened, and it was all he could do not to ravish her right here.

Instead, he went to the sideboard. He knew what he wanted to give her. Something special, magical. Something she'd always remember.

He chose a decanter of golden liquid and a goblet made of *atherias*—the magic-infused mineral that was the most valuable thing he possessed.

It was a deep purple with a faint rainbow sheen. He uncorked the decanter and poured the liquid into the goblet, holding it out towards her.

She reached for it, but he shook his head. "Wait for it," he said softly.

Calling on his power and hoping it would answer, he dipped one finger in the mead and ran his fingertip around the top of the bowl, as if trying to make a crystal wineglass "sing." A deep resonant humming sound came from the goblet, filling the room and vibrating in his chest, igniting a warmth like a tiny sun.

The sound intensified, and then a flame erupted out of the goblet, bursting into a golden sparkler. Trish gasped.

The sparkler burned for a minute or two, turning crimson and then deep blue before burning out harmlessly.

Trish laughed with delight, her whole face lighting up. The warm place inside his chest expanded.

"How does it do that?" she asked.

"Dragon magic." He smiled at her, his first real smile in he didn't remember when. It made his face feel strange. Her eyes changed as she watched his face, softening with some emotion he couldn't name.

"Here." He handed her the goblet.

She took the goblet and swirled the mead, which now had a sparkly sheen on top. "It's not going to set me on fire, is it?" she asked. "I don't have a dragon stomach."

"It won't hurt you," he said. "I promise."

She took a sip. He could almost taste it himself—like honeysuckle and summer, with the sparkles fizzing in his mouth. He hoped she liked it. He'd worked for months to get the recipe just right.

Her eyes went wide. "Oh my god, that's amazing," she said, taking another sip. "What is it?"

"Akhasa mead," he said. "It's a specialty of the Al-Maddeiri clan. I found the recipe in Marcus's library—the man who raised Kira." He added, almost to himself, "At least some of the clan's history was saved."

But so much had been lost. A whole clan, betrayed and wiped out in one day. Elders and children, customs, rituals, lore, magic, medical knowledge, food, drink, songs, dances, music.

She seemed to sense his mood change and put a hand on his arm, just resting it there, not asking for anything or trying to fix him.

"I'm glad you saved this," she said. "I like it even better, knowing it's from your clan."

He looked down at her, sparkling and shining, a light in the darkness of his lonely gothic castle.

There was a drop of mead on her lips, and he ached to kiss it off, to taste her sweetness again.

To shove her up against the wall and plunder her mouth. He dipped his head slowly toward hers.

Footsteps sounded in the hallway, and a babble of voices. Fucking wolves. Trish started and stepped back, then turned to the door.

And Emon pulled his cloaking ability around him, disappearing in plain sight.

CHAPTER 9

Trish turned to see Mina and Noah Reilly enter the room, with their six-year-old son Brock. Mina was the head of the research team, and Noah, her mate, was an Enforcer. His official assignment was supervising the two security officers who accompanied the entire team, but Trish knew that mostly he was here because of Brock.

Brock was unique among shifters. His biological father had belonged to the only pack of predominantly white wolves ever known to have existed. White wolves had mental powers—healing, telekinesis, visions, mental telepathy, and the ability to erase, blur or retrieve memories. Unfortunately, along with these powers came mental instability, dementia, and insanity.

That pack had been decimated by shifter hunters, and Brock was the sole known survivor—Mina, still human at the time, had been pregnant with him when the pack was attacked. Though he wasn't a white wolf, Brock had enhanced mental powers, and he seemed to have escaped the dangerous side effects. So far.

Brock was a major component of Mayah's healing team—he had an uncanny ability to communicate with difficult or out-of-control shifter animals and heal them. Noah had objected to him coming to dragon territory, though, and when overruled, had flat-out refused to let him come without his personal protection.

Brock took one look at Trish and his face lit up. He raced across the room, totally unintimidated by the formal atmosphere—or the knives sticking out of the portrait.

"Auntie Trish! Auntie Trish! You're finally finally here! I thought you were never ever coming." He flung himself on her and hugged her legs, talking the entire time.

"This is a castle, isn't it amazing? It's very very big, and dragons live here. I'm helping one, me and Uncle Tristan. Her name is Mayah, and her dragon doesn't ever come out because it's sad and sometimes inside her head is very confusing. We're helping her not to be sad and confused."

Trish knelt down and gave Brock a proper hug, which he returned enthusiastically. He was one of the few cubs at Silverlake, and probably the sweetest, kindest child in existence.

"I heard you were doing that," she said now. "How is Mayah doing?"

"She's still sad a lot because we've only tried to help her five times so far. Her dragon won't come out but I can feel her getting closer. I want her to talk to me but she doesn't want to yet, so I tell her about Silverlake and my friend Michelangela, and about Ashley and Kira because they're dragons too. She likes that." He frowned thoughtfully. "I think she doesn't come out because she doesn't like the ghosts."

Ghosts? Trish gave Mina a questioning look. Mina shrugged. *News to me,* she mouthed.

"What ghosts, Brock?" Trish asked.

"The ones who talk to Mayah."

"The voices she hears?" Brock nodded. Trish said carefully, "I thought the voices weren't real."

"They're *ghosts*," Brock said. "They're there, but we can't see them."

"Where are they, exactly? If they're not in Mayah's head?"

Brock cocked his head, thinking. "I'm not sure. They're lots of places, I think."

This was making less and less sense.

"Why do they talk to Mayah?"

"Because she's the only one who can hear them." He turned to Mina. "I want to ask Prince Scary Dragon if I can have the fizzy grape drink. Can I?"

Prince Scary Dragon? Trish bit her lip to keep from laughing. Only Brock could get away with that.

"When he comes," Mina said. She turned to Trish. "Have you seen Prince Emon yet?"

"He's right he—" Trish looked around. Dammit. He'd disappeared again. Stupid wannabe ninja dragons and cloaking ability.

"Seriously?" she said to the room at large. "We're doing this again?"

"It's a game," Brock said. "He's hiding." He turned slowly in a circle, chanting, "Dragon, Dragon, where's the scary dragon?" He stopped suddenly, staring at one of the windows, covered in velvet drapes. "I see you!" he shouted gleefully.

Brock ran over and threw his arms around... nothing. The air in front of the drapes shimmered, and Emon appeared inside Brock's chubby arms.

"Nice work, kid." He low-fived Brock.

Brock said proudly, "He's a good hider, but I'm a better finder."

Trish, stunned, said to Mina, "Since when can he see dragons when they're cloaked?" As far as she knew, no one but other dragons could do that. Sometimes.

Mina and Noah looked as stunned as Trish felt. "No clue." She dropped her voice. "I didn't know he'd made friends with the prince, either."

"Color me unsurprised," Tristan said, entering the room. "Brock can make friends with anyone."

Mina and Noah, still looking a bit shell-shocked, were watching Brock as he leaned against the terrifying and formidable Draken prince, chattering away. "I went to the stable today and I saw a horsie. I saw two horsies, and one was very small and the man in the stable said I could ride it sometime but only if you said it's okay. Is it okay? And Tristan and I talked to Mayah today and made her head feel better but you weren't there, and she missed you. And I missed you."

Tristan was grinning. "Brock magic," he whispered to Trish, giving her a one-armed hug. "How are you doing?"

She murmured, "Okay, thanks to you. We need to

talk."

Tristan gave her shoulders another squeeze, and then nodded to Emon. "Your Highness," he said formally. Noah and Mina greeted him the same way, and then Mina called Brock over to her.

A servant came to the door and announced sonorously, "Dinner is served."

Emon came over and offered Trish his arm. "May I escort you?"

Everyone's mouths dropped open. Trish felt like the dowdy governess in one of her novels, singled out by the dark broody hero.

She took Emon's arm, muttering, "You make them call you Your Highness?"

"No," he said, starting towards the door. "They do it because they're afraid I'll eat them if they annoy me."

Trish snorted. Emon said, "Don't be too sure I won't."

"No way *I'm* calling you that," she informed him. "Especially if we're going to do that sex dungeon thing."

"If I get you in my sex dungeon, I bet I can make you call me anything I want."

That was a bet Trish was not willing to take.

The proceeded across the hall in a formal procession. Trish had thought it would make her feel stupid—her and Emon leading the way, followed by Noah "escorting" Mina, and Tristan and Brock bringing up the rear. But she found herself kind of enjoying it, as Emon seated her at the table and then stood at the head of the table, waiting for the others to be seated.

She should not be flirting with the Darkwing Dragon, she told herself. It was literally playing with fire. But face it, he was sexy as fuck, and she needed to make him like her.

Not to mention the fact that she liked him. Even if he was possibly a pervy stalker, who looked in her windows and appeared in her room without warning. He also threw knives at paintings of dead men, but that was probably a sane response, under the circumstances.

Trish was seated on Emon's right, and the servant showed the others to their places. The place across from Trish, at Emon's left, remained empty.

She wondered who was supposed to be sitting there, but Emon said nothing.

Drinks were poured, and then servants started filing in with the first course. Suddenly Tristan looked up, a slight frown between his eyebrows, his eyes going vacant as if he was listening to something in the distance.

Moments later, a woman appeared in the doorway, looking around hesitantly. She had dark brown hair that waved softly around her face, and green eyes like Emon's.

Brock sat up straight and smiled, waving at her.

"Mayah!" Emon immediately pushed his chair back and went over to her, taking her hand. "You made it. How are you feeling?"

She smiled up at him, but it looked like work. "Better," she said softly. "Still a little weak. Hungry."

Emon escorted her around the table to the empty

place and held her chair for her, edging a servant out of the way. He even put her napkin on her lap.

"I'm not a piece of porcelain," she murmured. "Go sit down."

He just gave a twisted smile, a heartbreakingly gentle look in his eyes. He touched her lightly on the cheek before returning to his own place.

"Good thing you're not," he said. "Remember that time I accidentally dropped you over the balcony?"

Trish almost choked on her soup. "You what? Why?" she asked.

"We were playing Draken Wars," Emon said, taking a spoonful of soup. "She was an enemy spy, and I was dangling her over the balcony on the fifth level, to make her talk."

"And you *dropped* her?" Brock asked, looking fascinated. "I bet you got in trouble."

Mayah smiled at him. "Well, to be fair, I can fly, so it wasn't quite as bad as it sounds. But I wasn't that good at quick Changes. Until that day, anyway. Quickest Change I'd ever done."

Trish watched Emon's face as he bantered with his sister. She'd just learned something else about the Darkwing Dragon.

He might be dangerous. And he might be crazy. But he was still capable of love.

CHAPTER 10

Three nights later, Trish was working late in the medical clinic. She liked it here better than the main lab, where the rest of the research team worked.

She didn't really know any of them, except Mina. Three of them were specialists sent by the Shifter Council, and the ones from Silverlake had joined the pack only recently. Also they made her feel inadequate, with their advanced degrees in biochemistry and molecular biology, or breakthrough research in shifter biomagic.

Trish was just a garden-variety shifter medic, with a degree in canine veterinary medicine, some knowledge of healing magic and potions, and Physician's Assistant certification in human orthopedics, since the most common shifter ailment was broken bones.

She was also capable of doing completely illegal surgeries, most of which involved gunshot wounds.

But she had some of her own ideas about the Draken toxin that was their primary research area right now. It had been a priority for the Shifter Council ever since one of Ragnor's formulas had turned up on Earth, in an attack on a group of Wild Dragons.

It had been stolen from a company called Gen-X, who were famous for their illegal shifter experiments. Somehow they'd formed an alliance with Ragnor, and had been funding his 'research,' lending him computers and drugs he otherwise wouldn't have had access to.

Trish didn't want to talk to the rest of the team about her theories until she'd had a chance to run some more experiments. They'd probably just laugh at her.

She examined her petri dishes under the microscope one by one, each one with a drop of the toxin combined with another substance, to see how it reacted.

She really wished she could get a look at Emon's wound, maybe take some tissue samples to see how her ideas worked on a dragon already affected by the toxin. But the last time someone on the team had suggested the idea to Emon, he'd breathed lightning on the guy's laptop and turned it into a twisted blob of burned plastic.

They'd all taken that as a hard 'no.'

Emon had also apparently decided that Trish wasn't worth his time after all. She'd barely caught a glimpse of him since dinner the first night.

Trish, on the other hand, still couldn't think about the gentle way he'd taken care of his sister without tears stinging the back of her eyes.

Also, she couldn't think about that kiss without her ovaries threatening to burst into flames.

All in all, a lethal combination.

But she couldn't keep letting him avoid her. Pretty soon her injection would wear off, and She-Wolf would be threatening to bust out again.

She only had one more dose; after that Tristan would have to risk himself again to get her more. She owed it to him to try to talk to Emon before that happened, see if he could try to help her control her wolf without drugs.

Tristan had already tried, and gotten nothing but blood and bite scars for his trouble. They couldn't involve Brock; that would mean admitting to the Silverlake leaders that she was rogue.

Emon was her only chance.

After the visual inspection of her samples, she checked her notes on the infrared spectroscopy she'd done, and then went back to the mass spectrometer analysis of the toxin done by the rest of the team.

And then to the list of ingredients in Ragnor's notes.

Something wasn't right. There was an anomaly somewhere—the numbers didn't add up. It was like there was some other invisible substance modifying the mixture.

Like dark matter, in space. You couldn't see it or measure it, and the only way to know it was there was by its effect on everything around it.

But how could there be something in the toxin that hadn't been found in the mass spectrometry? Even if it was a substance of unknown origin, it should show in the results.

The lab was deathly silent. She really was going to have to bring in some music when she worked at night, or the quiet would drive her crazy...

And then she heard the sound. The hollow, ghostly

sound she'd heard the first night she got here.

And again, the whispering.

Moving as quietly as a wolf in the forest, she tiptoed to the door and peered cautiously into the hallway. No one was in sight. But the whispering sound was still there, faint and getting fainter, as if it were moving further away.

Trish followed it down the corridor. If there was a damn ghost in this castle—or a ghost convention—she was going to see it.

She heard it as she approached the stairway at the end of the hall, sounding like it was moving upward. Just when she got to the bottom of the stairs, it stopped.

Trish started up the staircase. She didn't know what was up here—probably nothing. The castle was full of empty rooms. But just before she got to the top she thought she heard, somewhere in the corridor above, a door quietly closing.

She stole down the corridor, trying to figure out which door it was. The first door she tried was locked, but the one across the hall opened. And on the far side of the room was a dark gap in the stone wall, where no gap was supposed to be.

A secret door. And it was open.

The secret door led to another stairway going up. Trish heard noises coming from above, as if someone were rummaging around in a room looking frantically for something.

That didn't sound like a ghost.

What the hell was going on around here? Who was

playing ghost, and why?

Trish went halfway up. There was definitely someone up there. She put her foot on the next stair and stopped.

Suddenly she felt like an idiot. What if it wasn't the ghostly person she'd heard in the hallway? What if she was barging into someone's bedroom?

She should be able to scent them, though, and she couldn't.

"Hello?" she called out. "Is someone there?"

Everything went silent and still, and then she heard a door at the top open and close.

She dashed up the rest of the stairs, catching a glimpse of a cluttered study as she raced across the room to the far door. It opened into a vast dim space, big enough for a dozen full-grown dragons, with a sort of balcony around the top. There were dusty human-sized tables and office chairs scattered around, though, as if this had once been used as some kind of work space.

There was no one in the room. Except...she bent down and examined the floor, taking her phone out of her pocket and turning on the flashlight app just to make sure.

The dust on the floor was scuffed in a pathway leading away from the door.

Ghosts didn't disturb the dust.

She turned off her phone light and rose to her feet thoughtfully, wondering what the person—or ghost—had been searching for.

And then someone grabbed her from behind, pinning her arms to her sides and lifting her from the ground. A harsh, raspy voice said in her ear, "Bad wolf. Breaking into locked rooms. What are you here for, Nightmare Wolf? Who sent you?"

CHAPTER 11

Trish made herself stay very still. There was a demon-possessed monster holding her, and his fangs were less than an inch from her jugular. She could feel his hot breath on her neck.

"No one sent me," she said, trying to sound soothing and convincing.

"What were you looking for?"

"Um…" she felt like an idiot. "A ghost?"

There was a long silence. Then the iron bands of muscly arms around her loosened, letting her slide slowly to the ground. The dragon turned her around to face him in the dim light.

No, not the dragon, she realized, looking up at his eyes. They'd gone human. Emon was back. She let her breath out in relief.

"A ghost?" he said, folding his arms and staring down at her skeptically. "You've been reading too many of those books."

She rubbed her arms where he'd pinned them. Luckily shifters didn't bruise easily, or she'd have mondo bruises coming up right there.

"It's not my fault this castle belongs in a gothic

novel. This is the second time I've heard a ghosty noise—a kind of moaning sound. Very freaky. And then this sort of whispering, like the ghosts are talking to each other."

He still had that 'you're fucking with me' look on his face. "Talking ghosts?"

"Chatty, even, apparently."

"And you're telling me the ghosts did this." He waved his hand at the room behind him.

Now that she had time to really look at it, she realized what a mess it was. At least, half of it was. Whoever she'd followed up here had been in the middle of a quick and dirty search when she'd interrupted them. Drawers dumped out and thrown on the floor, books pulled off shelves, pictures off the walls and flung haphazardly across the room.

"I doubt it. Unless they're poltergeists? Whose room is this, anyway?"

"Ragnor's."

That stopped her in her tracks. "I guess it wasn't him that did this then."

"Nope. He's dead. And gone."

Trish suddenly wondered what had happened to his body, after Kira had nixed the 'head on a pike' thing.

"Please don't tell me his ghost is lurking around in the castle."

Emon's eyes grew flat and hard. "Only in my head," he said. "And Mayah's."

Fuck. "Sorry," she said softly.

He gave a faint one-shouldered shrug, as if it didn't

matter, but she knew it did.

Emon went on, "This is—was—his study. Where he kept all the research no one needs to know about. I still keep it here because he was an evil motherfucker, and even though this shit shouldn't be out in the world, some of it might be useful someday against other evil motherfuckers. This room is off-limits to everyone except me, and nothing comes out of here without my permission. It's supposed to be locked by magic. So how the hell did you get in?"

He ran his hands through his hair, obviously upset. Now that Trish knew what was in this room, she didn't blame him.

Who the hell wanted Ragnor's research this badly? And who could have gotten past the magical protections?

Trish said, "It was open when I got here. I could hear someone searching when I came up the hidden stairs, but they ran out this door."

Emon gazed into the distance, narrowing his eyes. "Did you scent anyone?"

She frowned. "No. Which is weird, because I'm sure it was a real person. They left a trail in the dust." She pointed.

"What about now? Can you catch any residual scent?"

She shook her head. She could smell Emon just fine, but there were no other fresh scents in the room.

He said, "What about your wolf? If you Change, could you scent anything?"

"No." It came out a whisper. She couldn't Change. Just the word had caught She-Wolf's attention, and now she was clawing at Trish's insides, wanting to get to Emon. *Bite him. Kill him. He will destroy us.*

Trish closed her eyes. *Shut up. Shut up.*

"Are you okay?" Emon put his hand on her arm.

She-Wolf went totally still, the way she had when watching him fly the storm. The silence inside Trish was stunning.

She took a deep breath, looking up into his eyes. Then she slowly reached out and put her hand on his chest. "How do you do that?" she murmured.

He frowned. "Do what?"

"Make my wolf go all awestruck?"

Emon stared at her in surprise, and then gave a harsh bark of laughter. "How the hell should I know? Maybe she has a dragon fetish. Although people usually don't go awestruck until I Change to dragon form."

Trish had to disagree with that—she was feeling pretty awestruck right now. He was standing only inches away from her, close enough to see the flecks of gold inside the green in his eyes, and he smelled warm and spicy, like cinnamon toast, with a hint of smokiness underneath. She could sense the power and wildness of his dragon

"Don't sell yourself short," she said.

He gave another short huffing laugh, but the smile faded from his face as he looked down into her eyes.

Slowly, his hand came up under her chin, his fingers hot against her skin. "I see her inside you," he said softly, wonder in his voice. "Your wolf. She's beautiful."

Like She-Wolf, Trish went completely, totally still, inside and out.

Her wolf was wild, uncontrollable, homicidal. Rogue.

Few people had even seen her. No one had ever called her beautiful.

Emon was looking straight into her soul. Like he wanted to get to know her *and* her wolf, learn all about them. Her hand was still resting on his chest, and she could feel him breathing, feel his heart beating.

Faster than it should have been. Hers was beating like a triphammer, but she couldn't step away, couldn't move.

She-Wolf whined softly inside her.

Emon moved his hand to cup the back of her head, threading his fingers through her hair. Then he slid his palm slowly down her back, as if smoothing her wolf's raised hackles. He did it again, and again, and Trish gradually began to relax. She closed her eyes, feeling the tension drain out of her.

And then his lips were on hers—touching, tasting, exploring. He sucked gently on her lower lip, and a rush of heat burned low through her belly.

She opened her mouth to him, her whole being focused on the taste of his lips, the warmth of his hand on her back, the feel of his heartbeat under her hand.

He pulled her to him, deepening the kiss, a low rumble beginning in his chest. She could feel his shaft hard against her, and she was melting.

Inside her own chest a ball of fire ignited, as if his dragonfire was burning through his skin into hers. He rolled his hips against her, and lightning sizzled through her blood. He was darkness and danger, hard and broken, and yet he could be so gentle.

Something uncurled deep in Trish's belly, wild and primitive and wanting. She pressed tighter against Emon, devouring his mouth as he devoured hers. He nipped at her lower lip, then bit softly down the side of her neck to the tendon between her neck and shoulder.

NO! She-Wolf panicked, rising up inside her with a feral snarl, and Trish could feel the darkness coming for her. Her bones began snapping, her teeth bared, and then the Nightmare Wolf took her.

CHAPTER 12

One minute Emon was kissing Trish, and his blood was on fire.

The next minute he was faced with a snarling black wolf with feral gold eyes. They eyed each other warily, two predators: one murderously angry, one totally fucking confused.

He could sense her mind, but he didn't feel Trish. Just the Nightmare Wolf: black turmoil, and rage, and triumph.

Free.

The word echoed in his mind. Then:

Kill.

"Trish?" he said quietly, not moving, not wanting to provoke her into attacking. He could take a wolf easily, even in his human form.

But he probably couldn't do it without hurting her.

He reached out his hand slowly. "Trish? Are you in there?"

She couldn't be completely gone.

For an answer, the wolf lunged at him with a snarl and bit down on his forearm, ripping through skin and muscle nearly down to the bone.

"Fuck!" he roared. He shoved her away with his free hand and with his mental power. Her jaws loosed and she flew across the disused lab, skidding on the floor. She scrambled to her feet and crouched in the dim light, growling at him. He stared her down, bracing himself for her to spring at him in another attack, trying to call on his spotty and unpredictable magic for a stasis spell.

For a second he really thought she would take him on. Then, with another warning snarl, she turned and ran, streaking across the lab and out the far door in a blur of darkness, claws clattering on the stone floor.

Dammit!

He ran to the door but she was already gone, across the landing and down the main staircase that led to the Great Hall on the first floor.

He ran after her, but he only got as far as the second floor before hearing a huge crash of glass below, as she jumped through one of the goddamn windows and vanished into the night.

Moments later Tristan appeared on the stairs, his long blond braids half-undone and messy from sleep. Seeing Emon, he demanded, "What the fuck? Where's Trish?"

"Bounding across the courtyard on her way out to kill things, probably," Emon said savagely.

Tristan gaped at him. "She went wolf? In here?" He shook his head. "I felt something. It woke me up. But..." His gaze darkened. "What did you do to her?"

Kissed her. But there was no way he was telling that to Tristan. He didn't need another angry wolf on his hands.

Too late.

Tristan advanced on him, growling. "Tell me, you bastard!"

Emon knew he should calm the situation down; Tristan wasn't exactly the most stable wolf in the world either, and Emon didn't need two out-of-control shifters on his hands.

But he didn't care. He was a prince, for fuck's sake, and a Draken, and he didn't back down in his own castle.

<Snap him like a twig> his dragon said.

Great. That will help a lot.

"I didn't do anything to her," he said, getting up in Tristan's face. "I found her in a place she shouldn't have been. I confronted her. She went wolf, bit me, and then took off and smashed my window on her way out, thank you very much. What the fuck is wrong with her? And why didn't you all happen to warn me that there was an uncontrolled wolf here who's a danger to my staff, not to mention my livestock?"

Tristan snapped, "It's complicated. And this isn't the time to go into it. I need to go after her."

Everything in Emon rebelled at the thought of Tristan out there with Trish—saving her, coaxing her to turn human, holding her. Defending her. Being there for her.

He said, "This is my territory, and it's my responsibility. I'm going after her."

Tristan shook his head. "She knows me. I always take care of her when she goes wolf."

Always? Emon stared at him, eyes narrowed.

"Wait a minute. Are you telling me she can't control herself at all when she Changes?"

"No," Tristan snapped. He lowered his voice, glancing around as if making sure they were alone. "She's rogue. And if anyone finds out, she could be put down."

Emon's stomach twisted. Put down? As in killed? "We need to get to her."

"*I* need to get to her. You've done enough damage for one night, don't you think? I suggest you stop bleeding all over the floor and clean this place up, or everyone's going to smell the blood and want to know who bit you. Now get the fuck out of my way."

Emon didn't protest as Tristan pushed past him and ran down the stairs. Avoiding the broken glass, he went out the front door, turning wolf as he went.

Dammit.

Emon grabbed the neck of his t-shirt and ripped it off his body, wrapping it around his bleeding arm.

He muttered a cleaning spell and pointed at the splatters of blood under his feet. He hated to give Tristan any credit, but he was right. The last thing they needed was for the staff and research team to find the castle looking like a horror movie.

And start asking questions.

At least he could still do this simple spell. And this one—he summoned Tristan's discarded sweatpants from where they lay in the Great Hall.

He retraced his steps, cleaning up the blood as he went. Just outside Ragnor's study he found Trish's shredded clothes, along with today's pair of glittery shoes.

Purple. Her favorites.

One of them was half torn apart, the victim of her claws when she changed.

He picked up the tatters of the clothes, smoothing them as if they were worth saving. He supposed shifters without dragon magic got used to ruining their clothes when they Changed in a hurry.

But Trish probably didn't have a lot of clothes with her. And she loved those shoes.

It was stupid, but... Gritting his teeth, he tried a restoration spell on the clothes. To his surprise, it worked, even without his power enhancer. He folded them carefully and put them on the desk.

Then he tried the shoe. In a few moments, it looked like it had never been damaged. Absurdly pleased with himself, Emon put the sneakers on top of the pile of clothes, stroking the restored one gently with his fingertip.

Then he started cleaning up the study. Blood was spattered everywhere, from him flinging his injured arm around. He started the spell, then stopped and looked closer, small details registering in his brain.

Spots of blood on the desk and the file drawers were smeared, as if someone had touched them. And the mess in here didn't look quite the same as it had before. Things had been moved.

Fuck. That meant Trish had been telling the truth. Someone else had been in here. And they'd come back after he and Trish left.

They were looking for something specific—he just hoped to hell his idiocy in leaving the room open hadn't let them find it.

He cleaned up the blood in the room and reactivated the locking spell on the main door. Then he added another spell layer, dripping a bit of blood on the lock and sealing the spell with his thumbprint.

That should keep intruders out—assuming his magic wasn't totally fucked up. He picked up Trish's clothes and left through the not-so-secret entrance, double-locking that too.

Then he took Trish's things to his private room—one just below the roof that used to be a guard station. He tucked them in a cupboard to give to her later.

Now there was no evidence that anything had happened, except for the fucking window in the Great Hall.

He sighed, running his hands through his hair. In his state, doing that big a restoration spell was going to need a power enhancing artifact—and a lot of luck.

And he couldn't get it done before people found out about it—Grange or the staff were probably down there now, wondering what the fuck had happened.

He shook his head. Three days of virtuously ignoring Trish, and now they were neck-deep in each other's shit regardless. And he was still bleeding.

Heaving another sigh, he went to the sink in the corner of the room and unwrapped his arm. The wound was red and angry. Despite the continued bleeding it was healing faster than he thought it would, considering how much the toxin usually compromised his healing abilities.

He washed it out, welcoming the pain. He'd fucked up.

What was he thinking, kissing Trish like that? No good would come of it. Evidenced by the fact that she'd instantly gone rogue.

Kisses were supposed to turn monsters into princesses, not the other way around.

Apparently he was nobody's Prince Charming. No surprise there.

Either that, or his kissing technique sucked.

But now he understood what Trish had been hiding. Not just a monster wolf—but one with no Trish inside. This was who Nightmare Wolf really was.

A killer rogue with nothing to rein her in.

Since his sister Kira had mated into the Bad Blood Crew, he'd learned something about the things that could happen to animal shifters when they were traumatized. And on Earth, if they were so out of control they couldn't be stopped from killing, or they risked outing shifters to the humans, they were ruthlessly destroyed.

Emon felt like a ball of ice had splintered his chest.

That couldn't be allowed to happen to Trish. No wonder Tristan was protecting her.

Except Emon had the sick feeling that Tristan couldn't help her now. That something was wrong, and he needed to go to her.

What if she couldn't Change back? What if she got hurt or lost? Her wolf didn't know this territory, and neither did Tristan's.

What if she killed Tristan?

The towels were too fluffy to make good bandages, so Emon conjured another t-shirt, tore it apart, and bound it around his arm.

He knew he shouldn't get involved. He'd been telling himself that since the first night she arrived. Her wolf was crazy; they were both crazy, and he didn't know much about relationships, but he was pretty sure two crazy people shouldn't be together.

But he wanted to kiss her again.

He wanted to tell her not to be scared, to coax her back from the Nightmare Wolf, to hold her and keep her safe.

He wanted to feel the way spending time with her made him feel, just a little longer.

And he wanted her to be okay. Something inside him *needed* to make sure she was okay. He didn't want to think too hard about why that was.

He went up onto the roof and leaned on the parapet, looking out into the night. He could feel her out there, a dark star, her light dimmed.

It shouldn't be like that. The darkness shouldn't be allowed to eclipse the light.

She shouldn't be stuck with a crazy wolf.

<*The Nightmare Wolf is not crazy*> his dragon said. <*She is angry.*>

That startled him. *Why?*

<*Because the healer-woman put her in a cage.*>

That made no sense. They were the same being.

How could one cage the other?

I need to find her, Emon said.

<She will break you.>

I don't care. She's in trouble. Tristan can't help her.

<Elf Man is useless> his dragon agreed.

Emon snorted at that. Tristan did look kind of like an elf. Slender, blond, handsome, almost otherworldly.

<If you really wish to find her, I can do it> his dragon said carelessly, as if it didn't matter to him one way or the other.

Far away, through the darkness, he heard the mournful howl of a wolf.

Calling.

Knowing he was probably going to regret it, Emon climbed up on the parapet and jumped off into the darkness.

CHAPTER 13

Emon's dragon was right. It didn't take long for them to find her, even after she stopped howling. It was like there was a golden thread spinning through the night, linking them together.

He could *feel* where she was—near the edge of the forest. He tried to sense Trish's mind, but once again, he just got that jumbled sense of blood and rage and triumph and freedom.

She was still She-Wolf, and she didn't want him there.

But he was pulled toward her anyway.

He'd just reached the spot when he heard the snarling below him. Two wolves. Snarls and deadly growls, and the thud of bodies that told him there was a fight going on.

He dove down, a deathly shadow descending out of the night. He landed in time to see a midnight-black wolf ripping into Tristan's white wolf, her jaws at his throat. Emon could smell the blood, see the dark stain soaking his fur.

The Nightmare Wolf was trying to kill Tristan. Her friend—her protector.

Emon let out a roar that shook the forest. *Stop!* he demanded, putting all his power into the mental command.

Both wolves froze.

Back off! Change back!

He blasted the Nightmare Wolf's mind, just short of actual Compulsion. His alpha dragon dominance rolled out over her and into the forest. Everything went quiet.

Nightmare Wolf let go of Tristan's neck and edged backwards, every muscle resisting his command, her lip lifted in a snarl. With a huge effort, she rose to all four paws, tail high in defiance.

She *was* beautiful. Black as night, like his dragon, with only a tiny white patch under her chin. Regal. Magnificent. Pissed off as hell.

Emon's dragon stared at her, mesmerized. She stared back, her eyes shining gold in the darkness.

Dazzling, mysterious wolf eyes.

Then those eyes shifted to Tristan, trying weakly to get to his feet, neck still bleeding. She lunged.

DON'T KILL!

This time he blasted her with his mind and his magic, and she was literally knocked backwards, ass over teakettle, landing stunned twenty feet away.

He desperately wanted to run to her side, make sure she was okay, but Tristan was bleeding out. If he died, Trish would never forgive herself.

Cursing, he Changed back to human and went to Tristan instead, kneeling beside him and putting a hand on his flank to hold him down. "Don't get up, idiot," he said. "And stop struggling—it makes you bleed faster."

The wolf relaxed slowly. Emon examined his wounds. The Nightmare Wolf had torn him up good, and the bleeding was not slowing down. Fuck.

Emon was no healer, but he did know a spell that would hold the bleeding back temporarily—sort of a magical bandage. It would have to do.

He put his hands over the neck wounds, muttering the words of the spell, putting all his will into it. His luck held. The bleeding slowed to a manageable level, and then Tristan's body shuddered and Changed under his hands.

"Thanks," he whispered.

"Shut up, asshole," Emon said. "It's your throat, and talking makes it worse."

Tristan nodded fractionally, wincing at the pain, and then said, "Check on Trish."

"What part of 'shut up, asshole' did you not understand?"

But he got up and went over to the wolf. She was just starting to move, growling faintly. Emon put a hand around her muzzle, holding it closed. "Change back." He said it softly, but there was still alpha juice behind it. "Don't make me Compel you."

Those golden eyes gazed into his, the growl going quiet.

Then her body heaved and shimmered, Changing with a crack of bones, and Trish was lying curled up on the ground. She was wounded too, gouges from claws and some bite marks, but none were really serious.

Tristan had been trying not to hurt her.

She looked groggily up at him. "Emon? What happened?" Then he saw her nostrils flare as the heavy, coppery scent of blood hit her.

"Tristan," she whispered, a look of horror coming over her face. "What did I do?"

She tried to get to her feet and stumbled, knees buckling. He put his arm around her to hold her up. She was shivering.

Without thinking, he conjured warm clothes for her. It was a Draken trick—they could do it for themselves and anyone they were touching.

Trish barely seemed to notice. She just staggered over and fell to her knees beside her friend, reaching automatically for his pulse, muttering "I'm sorry," over and over.

The heartbroken tone in her voice almost broke his heart too.

Emon knelt down next to her. "He's okay for now. I did a spell to slow the bleeding. But we need to get both of you back to the castle."

Tristan whispered hoarsely, "I don't suppose you can do some of that wardrobe magic on me before we go?"

"Gladly," Emon said. "I don't need to see any more of your little wrinkled wolf dick than I already have. But stop *talking*, for fuck's sake."

Tristan smiled faintly.

Emon dressed him while Trish re-checked his wounds, still apologizing.

Tristan put a hand on her arm. "Don't," he whispered.

She stopped, looking down at him, biting her lip. "It's okay," he said. "I've been where you are. I've fought my friends, and bled them. I'll be fine."

They stared into each other's eyes for a long moment, and then Trish gave a jerky nod. Tristan squeezed her hand.

Emon, watching, felt shut out of their little circle. He'd never had friends like that, willing to bleed and die for him. Hell, he'd never had the chance to have friends.

Suddenly, there was a gaping ache in his chest.

"This is really fucking touching," he said, "but we still need to get him back to the castle. Like, now."

Tristan added, "Without anyone seeing us, if possible."

Emon grimaced. "There's only one way to do that," he said. "And you're not going to like it."

He backed up, and Changed.

CHAPTER 14

Be gentle, he warned his dragon.

<I am not a flying taxi.>

Don't be an asshole. And since when do you know what a taxi is?

<I am there when you watch those human movies with your sister and her mate and the panther> he said. *<Did you think I disappeared?>*

Just don't squash anyone.

<But wolves are so squashable. And they would make good snacks.>

Shut the fuck up and fly.

His dragon let him take control—reluctantly—and he carefully picked up Tristan and Trish, one in each forepaw. Then he gave a jump to launch himself, and flew back to the castle.

Once on the roof, Emon put them down as gently as he could, and then Changed and lifted Tristan up in his arms.

"This is stupid," Tristan whispered. "I feel like a cub. Or a bride."

"I'm not marrying you," Emon informed him. "Not even if you tell me you're pregnant."

Tristan snorted with laughter, then winced in pain.

Emon carried Tristan to his converted guard station near the roof. It was sparsely furnished, with a pallet on the floor, a table with a couple of straight chairs, and a few books.

He didn't spend much time here.

He deposited Tristan on the pallet. Trish was standing in the doorway, looking around the room. "You live in a castle with about a hundred over-decorated bedrooms, and this is where you sleep?"

"I don't sleep here," Emon said, checking Tristan's pulse. It was still weak and thready. Shifters didn't usually go into shock, but they could if they'd lost enough blood. Which he had. "I sleep out there."

He jerked his thumb toward the roof.

She stared at him. "You sleep outside?"

He shifted his gaze to her. "If you'd been kept in a cage for a year, you'd sleep outside too." He rose to his feet. "Besides, I'm less vulnerable in my dragon form."

He made Tristan's shirt disappear to get a better look at his wounds. Tristan tried to push his hand away. "I'll be okay now."

As if. The wounds were still seeping blood at a rate that was probably too fast for him to replace it. He tried to move Tristan's hand, and Tristan slapped his away. Emon slapped him back.

"Seriously?" Trish said. "You're having a slap fight *now*? Men are idiots."

"Fine," Emon said. "Then *you* get down here and convince him he's bleeding out. I need to get some stuff."

As Tristan half raised his chest and opened his mouth, Emon added, "And no, I'm not going to tell people what happened. Lie the fuck down and try not to die before I get back."

Tristan subsided.

Emon left him there while he went downstairs. He started for the magical storeroom—there were some potions in there that would help.

The problem was, they probably wouldn't heal him fast enough to keep anyone from seeing his injuries.

His steps slowed, and then he changed direction. There was only one way to make sure Tristan would make it, *and* possibly recover in time to keep this whole disaster a secret.

The Al-Maddeiri healing power. He didn't have it, but Mayah did. *If* she was strong enough—and lucid enough—to use it.

She was already awake when he entered her room. She ran to him immediately, running her hands over his arms as if checking for wounds.

"Are you all right?" she said. "I dreamed—I dreamed of blood and pain, and someone dying. And I woke up with this anxious feeling in my stomach, like it was someone I care about."

"Not me," he said. "I'm as okay as I ever am. It's Tristan."

Someone she cared about. Were they connected because he was her healer? Or was it something more?

That was a wrinkle he didn't want to contemplate

just now.

"What's wrong with Tristan?" she said. "Can I do anything?"

"Yeah," he said. "I think you might be the only one who can. I'll explain on the way." He hesitated. "But you have to promise not to tell anyone. Especially anyone from Silverlake."

She frowned, but agreed immediately. "Okay," she said slowly. "Tell me."

They left the room, moving quietly through the halls, Emon softly telling Mayah what had happened that night. "This is my domain, and Trish falls under my laws as along as she's here," Emon finished. "They both do. But if her pack finds out…"

Mayah nodded. "I understand." She paused outside the door to Emon's room and put her hand on his arm, looking up at him with her huge, haunted eyes. "I would never endanger hi—them."

Emon was about to push the door open when he heard Tristan say:

"We could leave Silverlake, you know. Go away. Work for Carmichael, maybe."

"As spies and mercenaries?" Trish said. "Even if I wanted to, he'd never take us with unreliable animals. And by 'us' I mean 'me'." Her voice was bitter.

"Well, the Bad Bloods, then," Tristan persisted. "Flynn's told me I always have a place there, and he's used to problem animals. If we were mated…"

Trish said, "I can't saddle Flynn with She-Wolf. He has enough on his plate. And anyway, you don't feel that way about me."

"I could do worse."

Trish gave a shaky laugh. "Than someone who just tried to rip your throat out? I don't see how."

Emon heard Mayah give a little growl beside him, but he was barely paying attention. He felt like someone had stabbed him in the heart. Mate Tristan? Shackle the Nightmare Wolf to someone who didn't even have the strength to fight her? Over his dragon's dead body.

He shoved the door open and went in.

CHAPTER 15

The door burst open, and Trish jumped. "Before you two run away together," Emon drawled, "you might want to make sure neither of you are going to keel over from blood loss. To that end, I brought help."

Oh, god, she thought. What had he done? She-Wolf growled, scrabbling to come out.

"Stop that," Emon snapped.

To her shock, She-Wolf did.

Tristan struggled to sit up. "I thought I told you—" he rasped, and then fell silent when he saw who Emon had brought.

The last person either of them expected—Mayah.

Tristan fell back on the pallet and turned his head away. "You shouldn't have dragged her into this."

"Why?" Mayah asked. "Because I'm a crazy dragon who's only fit to sit cooped up in my room while people probe around in the carnival that is my mind?"

"She can heal," Emon said. "You know. With magic? So you don't die?"

"I'm not dying."

Emon muttered something that sounded like, "If you don't stop talking I'll kill you myself."

Mayah walked over to the pallet, and Trish got up and moved so that Mayah could kneel down by Tristan. Trish had put a temporary bandage on, and Mayah pulled it away so she could see better. Tristan hissed through his teeth with pain.

"Well, that looks nasty," Mayah said. "I hear Trish did it. What did you do to piss her off?"

"Ha ha," Tristan said. "Of course it's *my* fault."

"Shh," she said. "Be quiet. I'm working here."

"Then stop asking me questions."

"How about *you* do what *I* say for a change? I'm enjoying being the one poking and prodding you, instead of the other way around."

"I don't poke and prod!"

Mayah rolled her eyes. "Does he ever shut up?" she asked the others.

"No," said Trish and Emon simultaneously. Tristan gave a faint grin, but he stopped talking.

Mayah laid one hand on Tristan's heart and the other on his neck. She closed her eyes.

A bluish-white glow surrounded her hands, spreading out in tendrils to all the places Tristan had been wounded. For a moment, every muscle in his body seemed to seize up, and then he relaxed with a small sigh.

Mayah's brow furrowed in concentration. The wounds on his chest grew smaller, scabbing over, though they didn't completely heal. The trickle of blood between her fingers stopped.

Finally, she opened her eyes. Tristan was staring up

at her, an awed expression on his face.

"That was..." He shook his head, clearly at a loss for words.

"You'll be all right now." She smiled down at him. "It takes a lot out of the patient, though, so I focused mainly on the neck wounds. The others will have to finish healing on their own."

"No prob."

Mayah removed her hands from his neck. The horrible wounds there were closed, and his color was normal. Trish's whole body sagged in relief. Thank god.

To cover her sudden rush of emotion, Trish wet a towel at the sink and brought it over. Carefully, Mayah began washing the blood from Tristan's neck and chest.

At that moment, there was a faint chime from Emon's pocket. He pulled out a small golden ball. "Fuck it," he murmured. "It's Grange. I have to answer."

He rubbed his thumb over the surface of the ball, angling himself so nothing else in the room would be visible to his Head Steward.

Everyone could hear Grange, though.

"Your Highness," he said. "I've been trying to reach you. There's been a security breach—one of the maids found a large window in the Great Hall completely smashed."

"Yeah," Emon said. "That was me. Nothing to be concerned about."

"Really?" Grange sounded dubious. "I was 'concerned about' a possible intruder."

"I told you, I did it," Emon said impatiently. "I

Changed in the courtyard, and I accidentally hit it with my tail when I took off. But there's nothing wrong with a little extra security sweep in the middle of the night. Carry on. Just stay out of my sleeping room by the rooftop. Mayah and I are binge watching *Game of Thrones* on my laptop. It has dragons."

He disconnected.

Tristan said, "He's not going to believe that shit."

"About *Game of Thrones*? It's true. Kira gave me the whole series on DVD, on account of I can't get on the internet without opening a portal."

Tristan rolled his eyes. "About the window. Most of the glass landed on the outside. If you'd hit it from the courtyard, it would be on the inside."

"If he's smart enough to figure that out, then he's smart enough to realize that nobody from the outside broke the window trying to get in, either," Emon said. "So there's no security breach. He's just going through the motions so he can say he did his job."

Except there *was* a security breach, Trish remembered. Somebody had broken the magical locks on Ragnor's study and searched it. Looking for something.

Emon seemed to be remembering the same thing. Their eyes met, and heat flashed between them. Memories of hot wild kisses tingled on her lips.

She-Wolf growled. *Out! Kill him!* Trish's stomach cramped, and a rib cracked.

Emon put his hand on her shoulder. "I said stop it!" His voice was low, but she could feel the authority in it. Stronger than Jace, her alpha.

She-Wolf stopped.

Tristan was staring. "Holy hell," he said. He looked at Trish. "Maybe we were right all along."

Emon raised his eyebrows. "Right about what?"

Before she could tell Tristan to shut the hell up, he said, "You can make She-Wolf listen. Any chance you're looking to form a crew? Or a clan? Or a kingdom? Whatever it is you Draken have?"

Emon's eyes looked like metal shutters had just slammed down over his soul. "No." He dropped his hand from her shoulder. "I'm nobody's alpha, and nobody's king."

He walked over and nudged Tristan's hip with his foot. Tristan immediately dropped into sleep.

Trish stared at him. That was one powerful sleep spell. But… "You can't just…do that."

Emon shrugged. "I only put him to sleep."

"Without his consent. And only because you wanted him to shut up. That's against the healer code."

"I'm not a healer. And this is my domain, remember? The only rules here are the ones I make."

"Don't let him get away with that shit," Mayah said. "Especially if you're playing cards with him. He thinks he gets to change the rules whenever he wants."

"I'm the Crown Prince." He smirked at his sister.

"You're a cheating bully," she said, but she stood on tiptoe and kissed his cheek. He wrapped his arm around her neck and hugged her to him.

"Is the Elf Lord going to be okay?" he asked. "I hope you fixed his dick when you were mucking around inside him. It looked kind of small and shriveled to me."

"You need glasses, brother," Mayah said. "His dick is just fine."

"Oh, gross. Don't admire guys' dicks in front of me. You're my little sister. You never even get to touch a dick. Ever."

"Of course not. I shall remain a virgin, pure and untainted." She waited a beat. "Whoops. Too late. By like three years." She winked at Trish. "Are you okay?" Mayah asked her. "Do you need any healing?"

Trish shook her head. "He didn't want to hurt me. I only have some scratches."

Mayah nodded. Then she said to Emon, "I'm going to stay here until he wakes up, just in case he needs anything."

Emon narrowed his eyes, but he nodded. "I'll call the kitchen and have them send up some food for when he wakes. They can leave it outside the door."

"Thanks," Mayah said. And then, when he hesitated, she said, "Shoo! Both of you. He needs rest."

After a minute's hesitation, they both left.

CHAPTER 16

Trish stopped Emon in the hall outside Mayah's room. "There *was* an intruder," she said in a low voice. "They didn't come in through the window, but they were here. Because the person who searched Ragnor's study was not me."

"I know," Emon said. "Don't worry about it. I have an idea who it might have been." He looked down at her, his green eyes concerned. "Are you sure you're all right?"

She nodded. "I'm fine." Some of the claw marks went pretty deep, but she welcomed the pain. Maybe it would make her feel less guilty about what she'd done to Tristan. "It's less than I deserve."

She hesitated. "I know this isn't your responsibility, and you and Mayah have done more than enough for us tonight. But...what are we going to do tomorrow? If anyone sees Tristan's wounds before they're completely healed, a lot of questions will be asked. I'm not just worried about myself," she added hastily. "It's Tris. If any of the Enforcers find out my wolf is rogue, and that Tristan covered it up..." She bit her lip. "He'll be in serious trouble, just for protecting me."

Emon blew out a sigh. "How long has this been going on?" he demanded.

Trish went hot with shame. A shifter who couldn't control their animal deserved to be cast out of her pack.

"Since Jace brought me back to Silverlake," she admitted. "Over three years. But it's only gotten this bad since the pack has gotten so big, in the last couple of years. Before that, She-Wolf never came out. She got suppressed when—" Trish shook her head. "It's a long story."

And she didn't have the strength to tell it now.

Emon's eyebrows were drawn together, his face dark with an emotion she couldn't read. But she had to tell him the truth.

"But once she woke up, she was completely out of control. And she's getting worse. You saw what she did to Tristan. She's a rogue, and a killer. And she can't be reasoned with; she won't even talk to me. It used to be when Jace was around, she wouldn't try to come out, but in the last few months even that doesn't help."

"You keep her locked up inside you?" Emon sounded incredulous. And angry.

"What else can I do?" Trish asked. "I can't let her out. All she wants to do is kill. And if she kills one of the pack—or a human—they'll put us in shifter prison. They might try to rehabilitate her, but I'll never be allowed to be a healer again." She took a deep breath. "And if she can't be rehabilitated, they'll put us down."

Emon looked away, and she heard him mutter "fuck" under his breath. "You can't go on like this."

"I know," she said miserably. She needed to ask for his help—she'd planned to—but not like this. She'd wanted to do it before he knew how messed-up she was.

"Damn it," he muttered. He paced up and down the hallway, still muttering, raking his hands through his hair. She saw his eyes go dragon, and then human, then dragon. She began slowly backing up, ready to run if he lost control.

"Okay," he said suddenly. He stopped pacing, eyes human again.

"What?" Trish asked, startled.

"Okay, you can stay here. I'm nobody's alpha, and I'm nobody's king, and there isn't a pack here, but this is my domain and I make the rules, not the Council."

He looked down at her, his eyes darkening with intensity.

"Nobody can touch you here. Nobody can cage you. Nobody can ever hurt you. You'll be safe."

Safe. She looked back at him, totally caught off guard.

She hadn't completely realized just how heavy a burden she'd been carrying until now, when she got a taste of what it would be like to have it lifted from her shoulders. It almost made her giddy.

He was offering protection. A place where she didn't have to hide, didn't have to suppress her wolf. A place where, no matter how far She-Wolf ran, he could always find her and bring her home.

This was what she'd wanted to ask of him, and hadn't dared.

But...

"What if I hurt someone here?" she whispered. "Your staff. One of the other wolves, like Tristan. You won't want to keep me either. You won't be able to."

Unexpectedly, he pulled her into his arms, holding her close. "We'll figure it out," he said roughly. "We can be monsters together."

Together. She wrapped her arms around his waist, melting into the feeling of warmth and safety. It almost made it worth being a monster, if she could be one with him.

Finally, she made herself step back, even though it felt cold and lonely outside the circle of his arms.

"Thank you," she said. They looked at each other awkwardly. "Well. Um. I guess I should go back to my room and try to get some sleep." She tried to laugh. "Even though it is almost morning. And I probably won't. Sleep, I mean." She was exhausted, but too wound up for sleep.

But she didn't trust herself around Emon. Not after what She-Wolf had done tonight.

He gazed at her for a minute, then said, "Come on."

Emon ducked into an unused barracks room and grabbed a mattress and blanket off one of the bunks, hauling the mattress behind him. Then he took Trish's hand, twining his fingers with hers as he led her back out to the roof, and laid the mattress out on the stone.

"If you're going to stay here in my domain, you have to learn the stars," he informed her. He pulled her down on the mattress, lying on their backs with her head on his shoulder.

She felt so good next to him. That cold, numb place in his chest thawed a little bit more.

He shouldn't let it thaw. There would be pain when it thawed. But right now he didn't care.

Because his wicked, dazzling Nightmare Wolf was looking into the sky with awe. His sky. Velvet black and thick with stars. Emon pointed out constellations, telling her stories about the creatures they formed.

Not telling her that the brightest star was lying there right next to him. And he'd just bribed her to stay with an offer of safety that he probably couldn't follow through on.

The sky was just starting to turn light on the horizon when he finished a wild tale about gods and goddesses, with lots of illicit sex and jealousy and people being turned into *raka*, the long scaly river reptiles with dragon-like teeth and heavy tails that could smash through a stone wall.

"You're making these up as you go along," she accused sleepily.

"My domain, my stars, my myths," he said loftily. "These are now the official royal constellations, and the official royal myths."

"Yes, Your Highness."

She snuggled up to him. She was so warm, and soft, and wild, and she was going to destroy him. But what a way to go.

"You should stop being so sexy," she murmured.

She thought he was sexy? Fuck. This was worse than he thought. He was doomed.

<We can't help it. Draken are naturally sexy> his dragon said. *<We are irresistible to humans and animal shifters.>* There was a pause. *<Everyone, really.>*

I hope so.

Because he was about to throw caution to the winds. Even if the Nightmare Wolf attacked him again.

CHAPTER 17

Emon shifted position so he was facing Trish, keeping her cradled in his arms.

"If I kiss you," he murmured in her ear, "do you promise not to try to kill me this time?"

"No promises," she murmured. "Scaredy-dragon."

"Bad wolf," he countered. He kissed her forehead, then her closed eyes, one after the other. He let his lips drift down her cheek.

No snarls. No teeth. No fur. So far, so good.

He tangled his fingers in her soft, silky hair, like he'd been dying to do, and tilted her head back, capturing her lips. Warm, sweet, better than akhasa mead.

He could never get enough of this.

"I think you like bad wolves," she whispered against his lips.

"I think bad wolves are incredibly hot."

He kissed her again, deeper, tasting her with his tongue, possessing her mouth, her sweetness. She moved subtly, molding herself against him, and he could feel her soft breasts and hard nipples against his chest.

He felt the groan rise up inside him. His dick was already on fire, hard and throbbing. He pulled her tighter against him and she hooked one leg over his, so his shaft pressed right between her legs.

All these clothes between them, his and hers, and he was still almost ready to go up in flames. All he could feel was her mouth, her hands, the curve of her back as he slid one hand down to stroke her delicious, rounded ass.

He had to feel her skin. Right fucking now.

He slid his hand up inside her shirt, stroking the strong muscles in her back, her ribs, her abs. He cupped her breast, teasing the delicious pebble of her nipple, loving the way she writhed against him.

He kissed the side of her neck, her collarbone, pushing her shirt up more so he could feel more of her skin. It bunched up, getting in his way, and Trish moaned in frustration as his lips left her body.

Emon dissolved the shirt with his magic. Problem solved.

He slid his arms around her, her skin like hot velvet in his arms.

But she pulled back slightly. "Blood," she murmured. "Cuts."

Her wounds. Emon whispered his cleaning spell, magically wiping away the blood and dirt.

Now he could kiss her the way she deserved—collarbone, the hollow of her throat, her breasts. They were perfect, and he kissed each one with total intensity, covering every inch with his lips, licking and sucking her nipples until she moaned.

Every rib needed to be kissed, and every cut, scrape or scratch. Her breasts again, and then her stomach and hipbones. Her hands were everywhere—inside the collar of his t-shirt, down the back of his pants groping his ass, at the back of his neck running through his hair.

Every touch lit another flame under his skin.

He was high on her—her scent, her taste, her silky hair, her warmth, her arousal—everything about her pushed him closer to the edge.

He wanted her naked, right now, *had* to have her naked so he could touch all of her. She responded as if she could hear his thoughts, pushing her pants lower so he could kiss her hipbones, run his tongue along their hollows and down toward her sex.

She growled softly and strained toward him, raising her hips so he could push her pants down even further.

In seconds, he'd dissolved them too, and she was bare to him, skin pale in the moonlight and hot as dragonfire.

He had to touch her everywhere—he had an almost frantic desire to feel every inch of her skin, claim it with kisses, make it his.

Drive her crazy with desire, pile pleasure on pleasure until she never wanted to leave his side.

He kissed her belly, her thighs, running his hands down her legs, reveling in the taut muscles under soft, soft skin. It was impossible she should be so strong, and yet so soft.

He worked his way inward to her hot, wet core,

spreading her thighs and kissing her clit until she was making desperate whimpering sounds.

He added his fingers, stroking and licking her at the same time. She writhed under him, clutching his shirt, until she went over the edge, her orgasm taking her in waves.

He rested his head on her stomach, stroking her sex until the aftershocks subsided, and then slowly began building her up again.

He kissed his way upward, one hand still between her legs, leaning on the other elbow as he kissed her breasts, her neck, her lips.

Her hands were at his zipper, opening his pants and finally, finally wrapping around his shaft. Emon growled deep in his throat, a dragon's rumble, but his beast was staying inside, like hers. No danger tonight.

Trish stroked him, sending waves of sensation up his spine, shoving at his pants so she could touch all of him.

Goodbye to the pants.

And then her hands were on his shaft, cupping his balls, and her lips were on his neck, kissing and biting, bitey wolf, he loved his sexy bitey wolf.

She pushed her hand up under his shirt, and it rucked up, exposing his wound. Her fingers brushed over it, and he flinched back.

The familiar pain that had faded to the background flared suddenly, and he grabbed her wrist, stopping her from touching it.

Trish froze.

He couldn't stand for her to touch that part of him. He didn't even want her to see it. Hideous, gaping, oozing—a huge patch of skin burned away and the exposed flesh poisoned. A reminder of his ugliness, his despair.

She raised her gaze to his, eyes wide, and he begged her silently to let it go, leave this alone, pretend it wasn't there.

Instead, still holding his gaze, she gently pulled his shirt back down over the wound, resting her hand on the hem of it, just over his hip.

Then she did something he'd never have expected in a dragon's lifetime. She slid down and dropped a feather-light kiss over the wound. Then she moved up and wrapped her arms around him, body to body, and kissed him deeply on the mouth.

The lump of ice in his chest cracked open, and golden starlight spread through him, followed by a desire so intense it dwarfed everything that came before. With a groan, he rolled her on her back and buried himself deep inside her.

For a moment he couldn't move. The feel of her surrounding him was so intense he felt like he was going to explode.

Trish made a small, utterly sexy sound and wrapped her legs around him, pulling him deeply inside her, one arm around his neck, one around his hips.

When he was sure he wasn't going to send them both up in a pillar of flames, Emon pulled partway out and thrust in again.

Stars and comets and molten lava. And feelings—feelings forgotten, feelings he didn't know he had, barreling down on him like a river in flood. A force of nature, unstoppable, inescapable.

He knew when they reached him, he would be destroyed.

He thrust into her again and again, trying to stay ahead of the flood, trying to lose himself in the intensity of the pleasure.

But as the pleasure rose, the flood grew closer. He thrust into her faster and harder, and she moaned and met him thrust for thrust, welcoming him in, deeper and deeper inside her.

And still there was no escape.

He threw his head back, desperate for release, for escape, for her warmth and sweetness, for everything he'd missed in his life.

And then everything coalesced at the base of his spine, shining star turned supernova, shattering him into separate molecules and sending him out into space.

The flood swept him away, and he was lost.

CHAPTER 18

Emon lay on the rooftop, Trish tucked into the curve of his shoulder as she slept, her hair spreading like satin across his arm.

Blue lightning danced around them, outlining their bodies. As it flickered back and forth, around and around, he could feel it binding them together, weaving together their hearts and souls and bodies.

Like a breathtaking magical net.

<*A cage.*>

He could feel his dragon pushing back against the bond, wanting to get out. Already trying to break free.

Because binding people to you, being bound to them with love or magic or responsibility, *was* a cage. No freedom. No escape.

And she would die, because she was a wolf, with a normal lifespan. Or he would die first, of his wound, and leave her heart torn in two. Or he'd live, which would be even worse.

Centuries, alone in his cage. Never to find happiness with anyone else.

He couldn't let this happen. To either of them.

Emon pressed his lips to Trish's forehead, using his

magic to push her into an even deeper sleep. Then he got up quietly, tucked the blanket gently around her, and left.

The lightning flickered out.

He went down the steps and looked into his room, but Tristan and Mayah were both gone, along with the bloodstained towels. Nothing to show that a bleeding, half-dead wolf had ever been here.

Now, where the hell had they gone?

He checked Mayah's room, expecting to find it dim and shuttered as usual. To his surprise, the windows were open, letting in light and fresh air, and Mayah was in front of the long mirror, piling her hair on top of her head and turning this way and that to see how it looked.

Instead of the drab baggy clothes she usually wore, she had on snug jeans and a top with a peacock feather design. Three or four discarded outfits were scattered on the bed, which had been made.

For the first time in months.

Emon felt equal parts pleased and disturbed. Pleased that she seemed to be taking an interest in life—and her appearance.

Disturbed because he was getting an inkling as to why.

Emon said, "Where's the languishing Elf Lord?"

Mayah rolled her eyes at him in the mirror. "Could you say that a little louder? I think only half the castle heard you."

Emon grimaced. "There's no one around. And they

wouldn't know who I meant anyway." But he came inside and shut the door.

Mayah found a style she seemed to like and began pinning her hair up. "I put him in one of the unused bedrooms on the third floor. No one ever goes there. I left a message for the healing team that I'd told Tristan I decided to take a day off from treatment, so he went for a run as a wolf."

"Not a bad story," Emon acknowledged. "Is he okay?"

She nodded. "Everything's healing up. He should be able to come out by tomorrow. Tonight, if he doesn't get too close to people."

Emon nodded, relief spreading through him. Trish would be safe. No one would find out what she'd done.

"How are you feeling?" he asked, tugging on one of the wavy strands of hair Mayah was pulling out of her hairdo to frame her face. "You look better than I expected. That was a pretty big healing you did last night, and you're not used to it."

In fact, she looked fantastic. Color in her cheeks, and eyes sparkling. Again, those twin spears of happiness and disquiet pricked at him.

"Fine," she said. "Physically it was tiring, but..." She turned to face him. "Emon, you have no idea how wonderful it was to do something useful for a change. Instead of being the crazy one, everyone tiptoeing around me and telling me not to exert myself."

"It suits you," he admitted. "Maybe the treatments are working better than we thought, even with the relapses."

She shook her head. "I'd like to think so," she said. "But the nightmares I've been getting, the visions, they're so strange—and they come on so suddenly. They're different from before. You know—after we first got away from Ragnor."

That got his full attention. "Different how?"

Mayah sat down on the bed. Emon shoved a pile of clothes out of the way and sat down next to her. She said, "It's hard to explain. After Ragnor died, I still had nightmares about being in his lab. And I heard voices—people calling out to me. Like souls stuck in hell."

He put his arm around her shoulders and rubbed her upper arm. She leaned against him.

"These are more—psychedelic. Like some of the very first times when Ragnor had me in the lab. Everything's distorted, and the voices are so loud and I can see the souls that are calling out to me, but none of it's realistic. The people and things I see are strange colors, or they're all pushed out of shape, or I see things that don't exist, like pink-spotted wolves, or flying raka."

"And you never saw things like that before?"

"Like I said, I sometimes did when Ragnor was first experimenting on me. But this is even different from that. After the weird stuff, everything turns dark and scary and horrible." Mayah gazed into the distance. "I'm surrounded by demons screaming at me, or swarms of bugs that can bite through my scales and they're devouring me..."

She shivered.

Emon pulled her into a hug. "Sorry," he said, resting his chin on her head. "I didn't mean to bring it all back. Especially when you were feeling happy."

She shook her head. "It's okay."

Emon said carefully, "It seemed to me like it's been getting worse since the healers came." He hesitated. She was going to hate this next part. "Ever since Tristan started mucking around in your head. Are you sure he's helping?"

Mayah pulled away from him. "He's not making it worse, if that's what you're trying to say. He makes me feel better." Her tone was fierce and definite.

Oh, fuck. She *was* starting to have feelings for the Elf Lord. "Be careful, Mayah," he said quietly. "Don't get too attached. He's a wolf—and you're just a job to him."

She huffed. "I could say the same to you, big brother. *She's* a wolf too—and she's also here just to do a job." He opened his mouth, and she added, "And if the words 'that's different' come out of your mouth, I swear I'll flame you until your nose melts off."

His mouth twisted into a grin—or maybe a grimace. "Fine. We'll both stay away from the wolves."

It was better that way.

"Uh huh." Mayah picked up a red shirt and held it up next to her chest. "Which of these shirts do you think I should wear when I go back later to check on the Elf Lord's dick? I mean neck?"

Emon dropped his face into his palm. He was going to have to invent another god or goddess for his royal pantheon in the stars. One that was the patron god of hopeless causes. Because that's what the prince and princess of Al-Maddeiri were.

Hopeless.

CHAPTER 19

Emon left Mayah, feeling even more unhappy and unsettled inside.

He started for the dining room, and then he changed his mind and headed for his study. And then he somehow found himself heading back to the roof, even though everything inside him told him he shouldn't.

But she wasn't there. The mattress was still there, but the blanket was gone. The rooftop was empty — except for the little boy sitting on top of the parapet on the far side of the roof, legs dangling, looking out at the valley.

Emon went over. "Hey, Brock," he said. "What are you doing up here?" He couldn't remember ever seeing him on the roof before.

"I don't know," Brock said matter-of-factly. "Something inside me told me I should come up here, so I came."

Huh. Emon went over and leaned his elbows on the parapet next to him.

After a minute Brock moved over and leaned against his shoulder. "You're sad," he said. "And confused in your head."

Emon thought about denying it, but what the hell. The kid could reach inside his mind; he'd know he was lying.

"Yeah," he said.

Brock nodded. "Your dragon is mad at stuff. And he's scared."

Scared? No. "That'll be the day."

Brock shook his head. "Nope, he is. But he's like my friend Xander Grumpy Panther, or my other friend Mr. Flynn Roary Lion. They don't like to be scared so they get mad instead. Then they fight with people. Xander even wants to kill things lots of times."

That was true. Emon knew both Flynn and Xander.

Emon's dragon said to Brock, <*Are you suggesting I fight you? Because I would probably step on you by mistake and squash you. But we can try, if you wish.*>

Brock laughed. "You're right, I'm not big enough to fight very good yet. I'm only six."

<*I will fight you when you grow up, then.*>

Brock rested his head on Emon's shoulder. "Can I tell you and your dragon a secret? I don't really like to fight anyway. But when I'm really mad, my woof likes to kill rabbits and eat them all up. Maybe that would make you feel better too."

He paused thoughtfully. "Except, you'd prob'ly need to kill something bigger. A sheep or a deer." He elbowed Emon and added, "Be careful not to step on it though, or you'll have to lick it off the ground like jelly."

That made Emon laugh.

<*I can still eat you, even if we don't fight*> his dragon

said. <*You probably taste bad though.*>

Brock said, "No, I don't think little boy woofs taste very good. And anyways," he added casually, "I know you wouldn't eat me really because inside you're a good dragon. You're very fierce, like Kira the Warrior Princess, and grumpy like Mr. Flynn Roary Lion and Xander, but you're good on your insides like they are."

<*Don't be too sure, little wolfling.*>

Brock just patted his arm.

"So what else do Xander and Flynn do when they're mad?" Emon asked, fascinated by Brock's take on the Bad Blood Crew.

Brock thought about that. "They don't get mad as much, now that they have mates. Their mates hug them and love them lots, and then they feel better inside. Mates are magic. I'm thinking your dragon needs a mate."

Emon felt like he'd been wandering through a field of wildflowers, and one of them had just reached up and stabbed him in the stomach. Even this little kid was trying to cage him.

<*He is only a wolfling. He knows nothing.*>

Emon said kindly, "Well, there aren't any female dragons around here that I'm not related to, so I'm thinking that probably won't work for me."

Brock said, "A dragon would be nice, but she wouldn't *have* to be one. She could be a human or a panther or a wolf or anything."

Emon felt the need to explain the facts of life to Brock. He seemed to live in a fairyland where everybody could be happy. "If she wasn't a dragon, she would die a long time before I would," he pointed out. "Then my dragon would be alone and sad for a long time."

Worse than now, he almost said.

There was more silence while Brock contemplated that. Then he shook his head. "Mr. Flynn Roary Lion and Mr. Israel Magic Wolf mated with dragons. And they got dragon magic and now they'll live a long time like their mates."

Emon had forgotten that—if he'd ever paid attention to it in the first place. "Who says?" he asked carefully.

Brock shrugged. "*Everybody* knows that. But Pretty Princess Ashley said she would have mated with Israel Magic Wolf anyway because it would have been the best eighty years of her life and she would have been very sad without him."

He picked up a pebble from the top of the parapet and dropped it over, watching it fall to the ground five levels below. "I always thought having a mate would be nice, when I grow up," he added. "Like having someone who's your best friend around all the time. And if they're a true mate, they always love you a lot, so you're never by yourself really, even when they're not there."

You're never by yourself really, even when they're not there.

Emon stood in the sunshine, Brock leaning on his shoulder, and somehow he really did start to feel better, even though his insides were still churning.

Finally he straightened up. "I think my dragon needs to go flying," he told Brock.

The little boy nodded. "And maybe kill something and eat it up?"

Emon huffed a short laugh. "Yeah. Maybe."

"Okay." Brock spun around and jumped off the parapet onto the rooftop. "I have to go eat breakfast." He paused and asked, "Can I see your dragon?"

Seriously? Clearly, the kid did not know what he was asking.

"I'm not sure that's a good idea…" he began.

<*I will not eat him just now*> his dragon assured him. <*He amuses me.*>

Brock was just standing, waiting.

You better mean that, Emon said to his dragon. Then he backed up and Changed.

Brock's eyes grew to be about the size of dinner plates. "Wowie zowie," he said. "You are super-awesome, Prince Scary Dragon. I really like your scales and your claws and your tail and everything!"

<*Of course I am super-awesome. It goes without saying. But you may say it anyway.*>

He curved his neck, bringing his head down toward the little boy. It was bigger than he was, but Brock didn't seem at all intimidated.

And then Emon's dragon took control and…licked him? WTF?

Brock went into a fit of giggles, wiping his cheek with his hand.

<*You're right*> the dragon said loftily. <*Little wolflings do not taste good.*>

That just made Brock giggle harder. And then he

freaking patted the Darkwing Dragon's nose, like he was a pony.

And he still did not get eaten.

"I knew you were a good dragon," Brock said. "I have to go. Thank you for showing yourself to me."

He ran off toward the stairs. Halfway there, he turned and called out, "Good hunting!"

Emon shook his head, and then jumped off the roof into the cool morning air.

CHAPTER 20

Emon flew out over his domain, still thinking about Brock. He'd never met anyone like him; he seemed to glow from the inside with a pure, bright light. Just being next to him had made Emon feel like everything might somehow work out okay.

Even though it probably wouldn't.

But he couldn't stop replaying what Brock had said, no matter how hard he tried not to.

Because even if Trish wanted to live as long as a dragon, it was impossible. Flynn was descended from the Lion Guard of Al-Maddeiri, and had Draken DNA. Israel Jonas had been gifted with Draken health and longevity by the king of House Akkabi.

This wasn't the same.

<*We are the king of Al-Maddeiri*> his dragon said. <*We could do that. If we wanted.*>

That wasn't as encouraging as it might have been; his dragon was convinced he could do anything, whether it was possible or not.

And it was stupid to make life decisions based on the advice of a six-year-old.

<*I think the wolfling snack is right*> his dragon said.

You do?

<Yes. We should kill something and devour it.>

Emon sighed.

He strained his wings, feeling the burn of the wound in his side but ignoring it. Instead, he climbed higher and higher, as if he could escape into the sun.

For the hundredth time, or maybe the thousandth, he wished he was the one who'd gotten to kill Ragnor the Evil Fucking Bastard, instead of Flynn. He'd still be wounded, but at least he'd feel better about it.

<It would be even better if we could bring the Evil One back to life, and kill him again. And again. And again.>

Yes, it would.

He could see almost to the edges of his domain now—the ring of mountains that surrounded his territory, the atherias mine, the gold mine, the iron mines. The castle, and the river, the long line of the cliffs with their waterfalls and fertile valley at the bottom, the meadows where sheep and cattle grazed. The farms that provided food and grain and cloth fibers and leather, the forests where they harvested timber.

It was a good domain, and a prosperous one. From this height, all the buildings looked like toys, and the people looked like tiny insects.

<Let's squash them> his dragon said.

Bloodthirsty beast.

You can have a sheep.

Emon headed for the pasture where his private flock of dragon-bait sheep were kept. Like the kid said, there was nothing like blood and death to pick your spirits up.

He gave one last beat of his wings and then spread them wide, spiraling slowly downward, his dragon thinking of hot blood and crunchy bones, and the taste of fresh meat. The sheep scattered as his great shadow passed over them, bleating frantically, but there was nowhere for them to escape to.

He was Death on wings.

As he swooped over them, he noticed a patch of white that wasn't moving with the rest of the flock.

He gave a flap of his wings, banked, and came around again for another look.

It was a dead sheep, huddled at the edge of the field near a tangle of underbrush that bordered a small creek.

Dammit. Another one.

Emon dropped out of the sky, Changing to human and landing on his feet a few yards away, and walked over to check it out.

<*It's no fun if they're already dead*> his dragon complained. <*They don't run.*>

Shut up.

The kill was fresh, no more than half a day old.

He squatted down, checking the wounds, and then turned the creature over. The flesh had been torn and gouged, but there were no bite marks clear enough to identify what had killed it.

He was so focused on the sheep that for a moment he didn't register the faint sound, barely audible over the burbling of the creek.

A high-pitched bleating—weak and exhausted, and yet still with a note of panic.

He rose to his feet and made his way to the thick underbrush at the edge of the creek. He parted the branches carefully, thorns stabbing at his hands.

Caught in the middle of the bramble patch was a lamb. The dead sheep must have been a nursing mother. Damn those Wild Dragons all to hell.

<*It's very small for a snack*> his dragon said dubiously. <*Do they make those in a six-pack?*>

Emon ignored him. The lamb was sagging with weariness—it had probably run away in panic when its mother was killed and been stuck here ever since, crying for help. When it saw him, though, its eyes dilated with fear and it struggled to get away.

Because everybody loves a predator.

Emon untangled the lamb, then lifted it up and cradled it his arms. The silly little thing was bleeding from multiple puncture wounds, and it looked like one of its legs might be broken.

He stroked the lamb's head, and it immediately changed its tune, snuggling into his arms and sucking on one of his fingers. It was fucking adorable. And probably starving.

<*Bring it out and Change so we can eat it.*>

He sighed. *We're not eating it.*

His dragon sounded puzzled. <*But that's what lambs are for.*>

True. More than one lamb from this very flock had ended up on Emon's dinner table, not even counting the sheep his dragon ate.

Damn all little fuzzy animals anyway. Baby things

were like that, sneaking up on you with their big eyes and cuteness. It was just Nature's way of trying to sucker you out of killing them.

And it was working. But what was he going to do with a lamb?

The answer came to him immediately. Trish.

<Mayah can heal it> his dragon pointed out. <If we're not going to eat it.>

She's tired from last night. And she won't know how to take care of it once it's healed. Trish would be better.

A bright shining star, that made him feel good just by being near him. She could make the lamb feel better too.

<She will try to cage us. Destroy us.> But his dragon sounded hesitant, almost unsure.

She wouldn't do that.

<The bond is a cage.>

Emon stood in the sunlit field, holding the lamb to his chest.

What if it's not? he said. *What if the bond could heal us? What if it could heal the Nightmare Wolf?*

<Nothing would be the same> his dragon said. But he sounded even less sure. <The prophecy says we will be broken.>

Trish is a healer. What if she can put us back together? Make us whole?

His dragon said nothing, but Emon could feel him thinking. He remembered Brock's words.

You're not scared, are you? he said. It was a cheap shot, but it worked.

<I fear nothing. That silly bond cannot hold me if I do not wish it.>

You're right. So there's nothing to be afraid of. Even if you were afraid, which you're not. So let's go see Trish.

Dramatic, dragon-sized sigh. *<If you must.>*

Emon set off to carry his lamb back to the castle — back to Trish. Apparently, he was taking life advice from a six-year-old after all.

Trish was in the med lab, pretending to work, but she couldn't focus. Last night had been an emotional rollercoaster, ending up with crazy hot wild sex that had done things to her she'd never even dreamed of.

She'd even thought, like an idiot, that she'd felt the beginnings of a bond with Emon. A deep, magical bond — the real thing.

And then she'd had a dream about a dragon in a cage like a laser grid made of blue magic. He filled the cage, and he was pushing against it, not even caring that it burned through his scales.

<She will destroy us> he'd said. And then he was gone.

And she'd woken up this morning alone on a rooftop, cold and naked, no Emon anywhere to be found. She'd had to sneak down to her room wearing nothing but a blanket.

And now it was hours later and still no Emon. No Tristan or Mayah either. Everyone had disappeared, and no one seemed to have given her another thought.

So much for bonding.

Just then the door burst open, slamming against the

wall like someone had kicked it.

And in walked the Dark Prince, looking hot and delicious and arrogant as ever, and he was carrying — not a bouquet of flowers or some other morning-after gift, but a blood-covered lamb.

Her life was not a romance, or a gothic novel. It was officially a farce.

CHAPTER 21

Luckily for Emon, Trish was in the med clinic when he got there. Just seeing her made something loosen in his chest that he hadn't even realized was knotted up.

She looked sexy as fuck—her hair tied back in a long smooth pony tail, her jeans hugging her ass perfectly, blue v-neck t-shirt under her white lab coat, showing just a hint of cleavage that made him want to kiss her right there.

<Bite her> his dragon said. Emon wasn't sure if he meant that in a good way or not.

He smiled, tentatively.

Trish did not.

"What the hell is that?" she demanded.

"It's an orphaned lamb," he said, holding it out. "And it's hurt."

"I can see that." She was already spreading a clean towel on one of the examining tables. Suddenly she stopped and impaled him with her gaze. "You didn't eat its mother, did you?"

Emon gaped at her. "Of course I didn't."

<It had been dead too long> his dragon added.

Emon ignored him. "I think one of the Wild Dragons from up at the mine killed her."

That startled her. "You have other dragons living here?"

"Well, yeah." It hadn't occurred to him that she didn't know. "There's a vein of a rare mineral in the mountains that can only be mined by dragons. They're...parolees, I guess you'd call them? I don't exactly invite them over for dinner."

"Maybe you should," she said as he laid the lamb down on the table. "Then they wouldn't eat your sheep."

She'd clearly never met Zakerek.

He watched as she began examining the lamb, her hands deft and gentle. Emon remembered the feel of them on his skin, the feel of her lips, and he was attacked with a deep surge of longing.

But even though he was right next to her, it felt like she was a million miles away.

She walked away to get some gauze and disinfectant, and his whole body felt cold. He wanted to pull her to him and make the warmth come back, but she wouldn't even look at him.

All her attention was on the lamb. She began dabbing the lamb's cuts with disinfectant. It struggled, and Emon put his hand gently on its head, stroking its ears. It settled down, sucking on his finger.

Trish snorted. "Apparently, it thinks you're it's mommy. Try to keep it calm while I treat it, would you?"

He kept stroking the lamb, trying to think of something to say that wasn't idiotic. And wouldn't piss her off more.

Nope. Nothin'.

Trish was quiet for a few minutes, cleaning the lamb's wounds and bandaging some of the deeper ones. She felt its legs and seemed to decide the hurt leg wasn't broken, but she put a tiny support bandage on it.

Finally she said, "You walked all the way here from the field with him?"

It was only a mile or so. "Yeah."

Trish flicked him a sidelong glance. "The farm would have been closer."

"Yeah."

"Or, Mayah could have fixed him all up with her insta-healing."

"I guess."

"But you brought him to me instead."

"Yeah..." Too late, he saw where this was going.

"Why?" She'd finished cleaning the lamb, and stared right at him.

She was angry. He could see it in her eyes, feel it in her body. Angry, and hurt. And...

He remembered what Brock had said, and forced himself to see further.

She was afraid.

Afraid he didn't care about her? Or worse, afraid he *did* care about her, but not enough to risk allowing himself to bond to her.

He suddenly realized how much that must hurt her, and he felt like shit. He had to fix this, because Trish hurting was like spikes being driven into his flesh.

He'd been right all along—that ball of ice in his chest had cracked, and there was nothing but pain inside.

"You're a healer," he said finally. She didn't say anything. "And...I knew you could make him feel better. You always make *me* feel better."

When you talk to me. When you touch me. That part wouldn't come out of his mouth, though.

He was fucking this up. He didn't know how to not fuck it up.

Her hands went still, and he saw her close her eyes against the pain. He could hear her thought: *Not enough better for you to stay with me last night.*

That finished him.

"Hey," he said softly, putting one hand on her shoulder and cupping her face with the other, rubbing his thumb across her cheek. "I'm sorry I left you this morning. My dragon…"

He tried to put into words everything he'd felt, but there was too much and the words all clogged in his throat like a logjam in the river after a storm.

"You don't need to tell me," she said, dropping her eyes. "I felt it—I dreamed it. He felt a bond, and he rejected it. He thinks it's a cage. And he left. You left."

He could feel her heart ripping into little pieces, and he wanted to put them back together and hold them there.

"He's scared," Emon said. And then he forced himself to add, "We both are. But we came back."

She raised her eyes to his. "For what?"

"To tell you we meant what we said last night. That you can stay here. If you want. That we'll protect you, and keep you safe. And if you want, I'll try to help you and She-Wolf heal. So you can work together. And maybe not be so…murdery."

"What about the bond?" Trish said. "Your dragon doesn't want it. He doesn't trust me."

He tipped his head forward, leaning his forehead against hers. "*I* trust you," he said.

She shook her head slowly. "You won't even let me see your wound."

Trish thought he would leave then. She was pressuring him; she was asking for too much. She knew you couldn't pressure alpha males but she couldn't stop—her heart was already gone. She'd bonded with Emon last night, and she could never go back.

But she couldn't stay here if he didn't want her. It would break her apart. And if he didn't even want to try...

Slowly, Emon stepped back. He sat down on the examining stool, and then he grabbed the hem of his t-shirt and lifted it over his head, tossing it aside.

Trish's heart broke, and she wanted to cry. She knew what this meant. Forget last night. This right here was him stripping himself naked to her for real—showing her the ugliest, most vulnerable part of himself.

Most of his chest was—well, she'd thought her wolf brothers were ripped, but this was a whole new level of hotness. Muscles on muscles, all perfectly defined.

And then he turned sideways, and she had to stifle a gasp.

She'd seen a lot of wounds in her years as a healer, and she was good at keeping her personal feelings out of it. But this almost made her gag.

It was on his left side, the size of both her hands laid flat. Raw, red, oozing—pitted with craters as if chunks had been gouged out. The edges were crusted with black, necrotic flesh.

Ragnor had purposely done this to him. As an experiment, to see how much damage he could do without actually killing him. It was sick.

"Holy fuck," she murmured. "Has it been like this the whole time?"

"No," he said. "At first it was worse. Then Kira blasted me with Al-Maddeiri magic during the battle with Ragnor, and it got better."

This was better? She couldn't imagine how much pain he must be in. She wanted to just hug him up tight and hold him, but she could tell that wasn't what he wanted or needed. But she had to do *something*.

"Can I take tissue samples?" she asked. "For the research?"

He shrugged. "If you want." He clearly believed she was wasting her time.

She got some swabs and biopsy needles, and took samples of the secretions and tissue from several places in the wound.

Emon sat silently, looking off into space, his only reaction an occasional hiss of air through his teeth. When she was finished, Trish said, "Do you want me to put a bandage over it?"

He shook his head. "I don't bother anymore. It'll just come off when I Change."

"I'll do it anyway." She made a bandage with strips of gauze and taped it over the wound, smoothing the edges of the tape maybe more than necessary, feeling the warm skin and ridged muscle over his ribs.

When she was finished, he caught her hand for a moment, turning it over in his and running his fingers gently over her skin. At his touch, she felt that flame come to life in the center of her chest, burning brightly.

Almost like having dragonfire.

"Did you get what you wanted?" he asked. Trish nodded.

Yes. He'd taken a step towards her. Told her, by showing his wound, that he was going to try to open up. Try to bond. For her.

And no. She wanted to make that horrible wound go away. She wanted him to feel whole again.

"I'll make you a deal," she said. "I'll let you try to fix She-Wolf if you'll let me treat your wound."

Emon gazed up at her, those green eyes growing smoky and intense. His scent filled the air, and Trish felt her chest get tight. She put her arms around his neck, moving up between his legs so she could hold him to her.

She wanted desperately to try to fix him. To take away some of his pain.

"You can't fix it," he said gently, as if he'd heard her thoughts. "It's been over a year. My natural Draken healing didn't fix it. Healing potions didn't fix it, or Mayah's healing ability, or any of the spells we tried. All the Al-Maddeiri magic Kira poured into us during the battle didn't even fix it. Not completely."

Trish pulled back and cupped his face in her hands, the scruff on his face rough against her palms. "Too bad.

That's my deal, Mommy Sheep. Take it or leave it."

He gave a soft huff of bemused laughter, and then pulled her head down so he could kiss her softly. "Okay. On one condition."

She waited.

"You can't tell the others. I don't want the whole damn research team descending on me like a pack of wolves."

"We *are* a pack of wolves."

That got a smile. He was so breathtaking when he smiled. "I keep your secret, Nightmare Wolf, and you keep mine. That's *my* deal. Take it or leave it."

She was definitely taking it.

CHAPTER 22

After dinner that night, Trish was still working by herself in the med lab. Trying to concentrate, but mostly thinking about one enormous, maybe not-so-scary black dragon with emerald-green eyes.

Who exuded an aura of loneliness so profound it hurt her heart.

Who terrified the research team, and yet could be so gentle with a tiny lamb.

Who'd survived so much, and was so strong, despite his wounds.

And who maybe, just possibly, might be hers.

Cautious happiness fizzed through her at the thought. Her grumpy murdery Darkwing Dragon was trying his best to connect. To let himself care.

And he'd promised to try to help her and She-Wolf become friends. Or at least, not enemies. Frenemies.

But none of this would work if she couldn't help him with his wound. It was a constant reminder of what Ragnor had done to him.

She knew it made him feel weak, and feeling weak was the hardest thing for an alpha shifter to deal with. It ate away at their souls.

Like the wound ate away at his body.

After seeing Emon, she'd spent the rest of the day analyzing the tissue samples while he was off dealing with the business of his domain.

Apparently, she'd been wrong in thinking he spent his days snuggling a hoard and brooding. He actually worked for a living, running his tiny little country. Well, okay. He did brood during his breaks.

She hoped one day he wouldn't need to do that anymore.

She'd put the samples through every test she knew, comparing them to the tests she'd done on the toxin itself, still looking for the missing piece.

Now she peered through the microscope, trying to figure out what was nagging at her. Within the tissue, the toxin was reacting less like a chemical substance and more like ultra-resistant bacteria or parasite. Worse—something that was not only alive, but that didn't seem to have a natural life cycle. It just kept replicating forever, feeding on its host. Like a cancer.

Unless…

Just as a glimpse of an idea flashed through her mind, something raised the hairs on the back of her neck, her wolf-senses going into overdrive. Danger, hiding in the shadows.

She froze, almost holding her breath, listening with her whole body. There was no sound, not even someone breathing, but there was that ghostly sense of presence she'd felt before.

She headed quietly toward the door, instinctively

keeping to the perimeter of the room, so there was always a wall at her back. "Is someone there?" she called out. She stopped moving, listening again.

Nothing. And yet...something.

"Hello?" she called, more softly.

"Yeah, hey there." The voice was so loud and normal it startled her. She heard footsteps in the hall, then Tristan appeared in the doorway.

"Oh, it's you." Relief spread through her.

"You sound disappointed. Were you expecting someone more interesting? Bigfoot? Or your dragon prince, maybe?" He smirked at her.

"Wouldn't you like to know."

Tristan looked at her more closely, frowning. "What's up? You look spooked."

She shook her head. "Nothing. I just got this weird sensation, like someone was watching me. Kind of freaked me out."

She looked down at her arms. She still had goosebumps.

Tristan lifted his head and sniffed the air. "I don't scent anyone, except for you."

"Me either. Just too much time alone in the spooky castle, I guess."

She went up to him and pulled the collar of his shirt down, checking the wounds on his neck. They were still visible, but fading fast. "How are you doing?" she asked.

He put his hand over hers. "I'm fine."

She turned her hand and squeezed his. "I am so, so

sorry," she told him.

"I told you last night. It's okay."

"It's not okay! Tristan, I nearly killed you."

"But you didn't."

"Only because Emon was there." It still made her sick to think about how close she'd come.

"Yeah. Usually I can get She-Wolf to submit, either with my mental dominance or by beating the crap out of her. But not last night. Got to admit, I was not sad when Emon intervened."

"I know. What happened this time?"

"I'm not sure. She was bigger, for one thing. And more dominant."

Trish stared at him. "I—she what? How does that even happen?" Shifters didn't just...*grow*.

He shook his head. "I don't know. Because she's been suppressed? Or maybe something to do with being around the dragons? Or away from her alpha? There's no way to tell. But it does mean that Emon is probably the only one who can handle her anymore." He hesitated, then said, "I don't think you can go back to Silverlake."

That hit her like a punch in the stomach. Even though she'd been planning to stay here, at least for a while, hearing that she had no choice was a whole different thing. Silverlake was her pack. Her home.

She suddenly knew what Emon meant about feeling caged.

This isn't a cage, she reminded herself. *And neither is a bond. Didn't you just tell Emon that this morning?*

"Emon said I can stay here," she said. "He promised he'd take me under his protection. He'll help me with She-Wolf."

Tristan's face lit up. "He did? He will? That's fantastic." He looked at her face, then tilted his head and narrowed his eyes. "You two have a thing, don't you?"

She bit her lip, not answering.

"Shit, you do." He shook his head. "You and the fucking Darkwing Dragon. Who'd have thunk it?"

"It's not anything yet," she said, smacking him on the arm. "If you tell anyone, I'll bite you. And if you say anything in front of him, I'll bite you more."

He held up his hands, laughing. "Fine, okay." Then, more seriously, "I'm happy for you. I hope it works out."

"Me too." She dropped her eyes, toying with the button on her lab coat. "Look, Tris—"

"What?"

"I just want you to know…this doesn't mean I don't appreciate everything you've done for me. I know the risks you've taken. I owe you more than I can ever repay. It's just…" She didn't know how to finish.

Tristan gazed at her, and then said, "Sit down for a sec."

He led her over to the stools near the examining table. "You know I told you that when I was with the Bad Bloods, Tank used to watch out for me when I Changed?"

She nodded.

He took a deep breath, and blew it out. "I never told

you all of it. My wolf used to take over, and I was in there, knowing what was going on, but I didn't have the strength to come back. Some days I didn't want to. More than once, Flynn came this close to having to put me down." He held up his finger and thumb about a millimeter apart.

"Tank was crazy too, broken inside, but that big damn grizzly used to Change and follow me through the woods, smacking me with his Frisbee-sized paw every time I tried to hunt the humans, or kill someone's pet dog, or head for the nearest cliff and try to fucking fly."

"Oh, Tristan," she said, putting her hand on his arm. She'd known it was bad, but not that bad.

He didn't look at her, just off into the middle distance.

"The Bad Bloods had this hut called the Crazy Shed. Reinforced, shifter proof, so when any of us got so nuts we were a danger to ourselves, we could be locked inside until we calmed down. But my wolf couldn't handle being locked in. So Tank used to sit across the doorway and talk to me. He'd tell me about all the stupid shit we did together when I was human, trying to make me remember and want to come back from being wolf.

"And with all that, the only reason he's not dead is because his neck is too fucking big for me to get my jaws around." Tristan gave a choked laugh.

"Sometimes when I was in the crazy shed I'd just keep lunging at him, attacking him, and he'd catch me and throw me back inside. Over and over, no matter how many times I bit him or gouged him, or how much he bled. He never gave up on me. *They* never gave up on me."

Tristan turned and looked at her. "I always wanted to be able to do more for you than I have," he said. "Not just because you're my friend, and I love your dopey furry ass. But because somebody did it for me."

Trish's eyes were filled with tears. "That doesn't make me feel better about what I did to you."

"I know." He took her hand. "I just wanted you to understand that I'm not mad at you. I've been there."

He scooted his stool over to hers, and she hugged him fiercely. "I don't deserve you."

"Of course you don't, I'm awesome."

She laughed through her tears.

Then he pulled back. "But in the end, the Bad Bloods couldn't give me the help I needed. I had to go to Silverlake and work with Brock and Rachelle. And now we have to face the fact that I can't give you the help *you* really need. We're just lucky Emon came along when he did."

"Yeah." She only hoped they could help each other.

"Listen," Tristan said. "I'm still keeping away from the rest of the team until all this finishes healing." He gestured at his neck. "So, if you really want to do penance, you can bring your laptop to my secret hideout tonight and entertain me with the latest movies you promised you'd bring here and have selfishly not yet downloaded onto my computer."

"Definitely," she said. "Should I try to scare up some

snacks?"

"Good luck with that." Tristan grimaced. "You can try the research team common room, but I'm warning you now that they wasted way too much luggage space on unimportant things like computers and chemistry equipment, and not nearly enough on junk food. It's pathetic."

CHAPTER 23

Trish arrived at Tristan's temporary room on the third floor half an hour later, armed with her laptop, a six-pack with four warm beers, and the lamest snacks in the history of movies.

Tristan was right, the luggage space had clearly been misallocated on this mission.

She knocked and then went right in, stopping short when she saw who was curled up on one end of the big upholstered couch near the fireplace.

Mayah.

Oh-ho. Was it possible this wasn't just a buddy movie night? Was Trish a wing man? Wing person?

"Hey," she said, trying to sound casual. "Where's Tristan?"

"In the shower," Mayah said. "He'll be right out. Did you bring the movies?"

"Right here." Trish patted the laptop and set it on the coffee table.

Mayah's eyes sparkled. "That is so amazing. All those stories in there, and all the other things it can do. It's like magic."

Trish laughed, surprised. "I guess it is."

At that moment Tristan came out of the bathroom, bare-chested with black pants riding low, his wet hair trailing down his back. "Hey," he said. "I invited Mayah to come."

"I see that," she replied. "If you'd told me you were having your weekly bath, I would have brought you clean clothes."

Tristan gave her the finger, and Mayah laughed. "Come here. I can help." She held out her hand, and Tristan took it. In a moment he was dressed in clean jeans and a green thermal shirt with the sleeves pushed up.

"Cool," he said, looking down at himself. "Thanks."

"I had to guess on the underwear," Mayah said, a wicked spark in her eye. "I hope you like boxer briefs."

"You don't think I'm tough enough for commando?" Tristan arched his eyebrow at her.

"I just think you should keep the jewels nice and safe," Mayah said innocently. "You might need them one day soon."

Whoa. Maybe he didn't need a wing person.

Tristan seemed stunned into speechlessness, so Trish, like a good wing person, jumped bravely into the silence.

She opened the laptop and fired it up. "So what are you guys into?" she said brightly. Yikes, no. Bad choice of words. "Movie-wise?"

Tristan seized on the lifeline. "What have we got? Chick flicks? Danger and explosions?"

"Both. So are you looking to stoke your manliness

with action/adventure, or are you willing to expose your utterly sentimental side?"

"Being sentimental is manly too," Tristan said. "Where have you been for the last thirty years?"

"Cool. Then we can watch a chick flick."

Tristan narrowed his eyes. "I think I just got suckered. I hope you at least brought the snacks."

"If you use the term loosely."

Trish put her warm six-pack on the table and emptied her carry bag. It contained a couple of mini bags of cheese puffs and a dozen individually wrapped sticks of beef jerky.

"Seriously?" Tristan said. "This is possibly the worst collection of movie snacks in the known universe."

Trish shrugged and sat down on the loveseat. "Talk to Mina. She's the one who made the supply lists, and totally ignored the snack factor."

"I'm sure this will be fine," Mayah said politely. She picked up a package of beef jerky and sniffed it, looking dubious. "Um. Is this food?"

Tristan just shook his head. "Here. Have a warm beer."

Trish was reaching for one when she caught a faint scent outside the door. Dragon. Hot, smoky, leather-clad dragon. And...

Popcorn?

Delicious, buttery popcorn. No way.

She saw Tristan's head go up, his nostrils flaring. Then the door banged open and a voice said, "I heard there was a movie party. Hope I'm not late. Did I miss anything?"

And Emon walked into the room. With one arm wrapped around a huge bowl of popcorn, and two six-packs of beer tucked under the other. Ice-cold beer—Trish could see the condensation running down the side.

"Damn," she said. "You're my hero."

He grinned at her. Tristan's mouth was twitching—she wasn't sure if it was amusement, annoyance, or the sight of the beer.

Emon stopped next to the couch. "Get the beer, Elf Lord."

Tristan pulled the six-packs out from under his arm. The popcorn bowl was nested inside another one, and Emon pulled them apart, poured half the popcorn into the second one, and set it ostentatiously on the couch—*between* Tristan and Mayah.

So not subtle. Trish bit her lip, trying not to laugh.

Then he grabbed one six-pack and came and sat down on the loveseat beside her, setting the other bowl of popcorn in her lap. He pulled a beer out of the six-pack, and opened it with and an honest-to-god tacky-as-hell bottle opener ring on his middle finger. He handed it to Trish.

"Where in god's name did you get that ring?" Trish asked, fascinated.

"Christmas present from Xander."

Trish rolled her eyes. "Of course it was."

"What?" Emon said. "Someone had to teach me the ways of Earth shifters."

Tristan snorted. "And you're relying on Xander

Fierro for that? He's a homicidal nutcase with a perverted mind. Kira must be laughing her ass off."

"Why?" Emon said. "He taught me about beer, football, bottle top flicking, and internet porn. What more do I need to know?"

"Not to get too full of yourself?" Mayah suggested.

"No way is Xander going to teach me that. Plus, I'm a prince. I'm pretty sure princes can't get overly full of ourselves, on account of how fucking important we are."

Mayah rolled her eyes. "At least Kira and Flynn gave us the mini-fridge and the microwave."

"I had to buy my own generator, though. To make them work."

"Cry me a river, sniveler." Mayah mockingly rubbed her fists against her eyes and sniffled.

Emon turned to Tristan, bottle cap between his fingers, a questioning look on his face. "Challenge?"

"Name it, sucker." Tristan took a beer and opened it by grabbing the bottle top between his molars and twisting.

Emon raised his bottle cap and aimed at the door. "Doorknob."

Tristan snorted. "I'm sure you meant 'doorknob from a ricochet off the ceiling', and not a straight doorknob shot a five-year-old could make."

Emon smirked. "Whatever, Loser Wolf."

Tristan put his bottle cap between his fingers, shaking his head. "One, two, three!" They both snapped their fingers, shooting the bottle caps across the room, bouncing them off the stone ceiling and down towards the door. One of them skimmed the side of the doorknob, and the other hit the base where it was screwed into the door.

"Tie," Tristan said.

"In your dreams, Loser Wolf. I hit the knob part, I win."

"Fuck you, Draken Prince." They leaned across and bumped fists.

Male bonding at its finest.

"Not so fast," Trish said. She grabbed a bottle and held it out. "Open." Emon, after a hard green glance her way, used his ring to open it.

Trish aimed carefully, then snapped her fingers and let the bottle top fly. It did a double ricochet, bouncing off the wall, off the ceiling, and then down to hit the doorknob with a satisfying *plink*.

"Woohoo!" She punched the air.

Emon's hands went up like a ref signaling a touchdown. "She shoots! She scores!" He bumped fists with Trish. "I can see you have many talents, Nightmare Wolf."

"I have talents you can only dream of," she informed him. She heard him suck in his breath. Yeah.

He wrapped his arm around her and snuggled her close, and they settled in to watch the movie.

CHAPTER 24

Trish tried to pay attention to the movie, but halfway through her wolf started to get restless. *Don't do this now,* she begged. *Didn't you cause enough trouble last night?*

Free, She-Wolf muttered. *Night. Kill.*

Emon glanced at her, then reached over and took her hand. She-Wolf quieted, but she wasn't happy about it.

Anxiety crept into Trish's stomach. If She-Wolf stopped listening to Emon, or even worse, started to resent him, this would never work.

Finally, the movie was over. Emon immediately got to his feet. "Come on, Nightmare Wolf," he said, putting the popcorn bowl aside. "We're going for a walk."

He turned to his sister. "And Mayah's going back to her room to get some sleep."

"Since when are you in charge of me?"

"I'm the Crown Prince—and you're not. And you're tired. Very, very tired. Plus, you need alone time. Extremely alone. No wolves."

Trish thought it was cute the way he was trying to keep Mayah away from Tristan. Though she had the feeling that was a losing battle.

Mayah got off the couch, though. "Bully. I'm doing it because I want to, not because you tell me to." She stuck her tongue out at her brother.

As she passed Tristan, though, she put her hand on his shoulder. He got a strange look on his face, and then a pair of boxer briefs appeared in Mayah's hand. "There, tough guy," she said, tossing them in Tristan's lap. "Commando. Careful of chafing."

And she walked out.

Oh my god. Had she actually conjured his underwear right out from under his pants?

Emon face-palmed, muttering about wolf dicks. Tristan was laughing fit to bust a gut.

"Goodnight," Trish called to Tristan as Emon pulled her out of the room, still muttering. "Wet—I mean, sweet dreams!"

From down the hallway, she heard Mayah giggling before she cloaked herself and disappeared.

"We should do that too," Emon said. "I don't want people to see a lot of coming and going and figure out Tristan's here. His wounds won't be totally gone until morning."

She felt a faint fizzle of energy as he drew a magical cloak around them, making them undetectable unless someone actually ran into them. Then he pushed her up against the corridor wall and kissed her thoroughly.

"Mmm," he said, his lips still moving down her neck. "I've been wanting to do that for hours."

Trish tilted her head so he could kiss that sweet spot right under her ear. She was buzzing all over. "What else do you want to do to me? You still haven't shown me the sex dungeon."

"It's under construction," he said, biting her neck gently. "Right now I'm taking you outside. Your wolf needs to run, and I need to try to talk to her." He kissed her again, lingering on her lips. "So come on."

Trish felt a trickle of fear. "So now you're going to boss me around too?" she said, trying to keep it light.

He nipped her neck again. "Yup. I'm the Crown Prince, remember? Actually, technically I'm the king. I was born to boss people around, and you're pretty much all I've got, besides Grange. Mayah stopped listening to me years ago, as you can tell."

Trish said, "Are you kidding? You have tons of farmers and tradesmen and miners and shit living here. Go boss them."

"Nah, too easy. All you have to do is dismember one or two of them, and the rest just turn into 'yes' men. And women. So boring."

"Ha ha. Very funny." But Trish was still resisting. She did *not* want to do this, did not want to give up control, did not want to be She-Wolf. Just did not.

Emon said, "If you and She-Wolf are ever going to get along, we have to start sometime. Come on." And when she didn't move, he added softly, "Trust me."

He was doing this for her. He was probably going to get bitten again, and bleed, and he was willing to try. Just like he'd been willing to take his shirt off today and let her see his wound.

The least she could do was try too. "Okay."

Emon knew Trish was scared. He could see it in her eyes, once they were out near the woods, away from the castle. Her hands were shaking as she stripped out of her clothes.

He went over and put his hands on her shoulders. "Don't worry," he said. "I'm here. I'll take care of you."

She nodded, pressing her lips together. He backed up a few paces, and she Changed.

The Nightmare Wolf sprang into existence, lip already lifted in a snarl. She growled, eyes on him, every muscle poised, as if deciding whether to attack or run.

His dragon rose up inside him. *Stop that,* Emon said. *I need to talk to her.*

<No. I will talk.>

He pressed at Emon, who finally let him have his way. He Changed into the Darkwing Dragon, and he and the Nightmare Wolf faced each other.

Then his dragon spoke. <*What is your name, fur-creature?*>

Emon didn't expect an answer. He didn't even know if she could hear his dragon when he wasn't blasting commands at her.

But her voice came into his mind.

I am Layla. I am She-Wolf. I am alone.

His Draken gave a snort, smoke puffing out of his nose. <*Draken are alone. You have a pack of fur-creatures.*>

They are not my *pack. The woman keeps me caged.*

<*Why?*>

She is afraid. She is weak. She is ashamed. I am a warrior.

She is not.

<She is a healer.>

She heals. I kill. She does not want me. She tries to keep me inside her skin, but she cannot. I am stronger. I come out, and I kill. Perhaps I will kill you.

The wolf cocked her head, as if deciding how Emon and his dragon should die.

His dragon gave another fiery snort. <I could eat you in one bite, and still need a snack afterwards.>

Layla was obviously unimpressed. *I would chew my way out of your belly, and you would die.*

This was one ballsy she-wolf. Delusional, but ballsy.

<I like her> his dragon said privately to Emon. <It's too bad she's not a Draken. Then she would be a worthy mate.>

Great. You could be the Bonnie and Clyde of the shifter world, going around leaving a trail of bodies in your wake.

<I liked that movie. There was a lot of blood.>

Of course he did.

Layla stepped forward, sniffing. *I bit you,* she said. *When you were two-legged.*

<You did not do much damage> his dragon said negligently. <It healed quickly.>

She sat down, her head tilted, tongue hanging out of her mouth.

But I did bite you. Very hard.

She sounded way too pleased with herself.

So what now? The black dragon watched the black wolf, two pieces of the night. Nightmares together.

<The night is made for flying> his dragon said finally.

The night is made for running.
<Then run with me.>

Emon let his dragon take the lead. He ran away from the woods, across the open land, with his lumbering dragon gait. After a moment, he felt Layla beside them, flowing like a shadow. Through his dragon's connection with her, he felt the wind ruffling her fur, the sense of freedom, the safety in the darkness.

The knowledge that no one could see her coming. She could attack out of the night, if she wished, or she could simply *be*, stretching her muscles, feeling her own strength, reveling in being *wolf*.

They reached the top of a little hill, and as they crested it, his dragon unfurled his wings and took off. And Emon felt it, their kindred spirits, as his dragon luxuriated in the wind under his wings, the stretch and strength of his muscles despite the pain in his side. The safety of darkness, being *dragon*, a creature of air and dark and death.

And life.

He swooped low, then flew upwards in a rush of wind and looped back, keeping pace with the running wolf. Layla yipped in acknowledgement, putting on a burst of speed, and Emon lazily loop-the-looped above her. They ran for miles, until the grassy plain ended at the cliff edge. Layla dropped to her haunches and panted, and Emon came in for a landing right next to her.

A round full moon shimmered overhead, and Layla threw back her head and…sang. It was more than a howl, it was a full-throated song—to the moon, and the night, and the sheer joy of being alive.

And Emon and his dragon raised their muzzle and sang with her, a dragonsong full of magic and promise and darkness and hope.

And when the song ended, he felt a cold nose against his front leg, briefly, and then, *I go.*

There was a shimmer and a faint cracking of bones, and Trish was on the ground in front of him, naked, her hair shining under the moon.

CHAPTER 25

Trish woke up naked. In the dark. On the edge of a cliff.

With the Darkwing Dragon looming over her. At least, he was for a minute. By the time she got her shit together, the dragon was gone and Emon was there.

"Where are we?" she asked. As usual, she had no memory of what had happened when she Changed. But she had a strange feeling of well-being, like she was tired but she'd used her body well. And she was... happy.

She-Wolf was happy. Trish could not ever remember that happening before. She hoped they hadn't killed anyone.

"We're about ten miles from the castle," Emon said.

His eyes were human, not dragon, but she could still see a tiny bit of lightning in their depths. "You're not bleeding," she noted. "That's a good sign. How'd it go?"

A breeze ran across her body, and Trish felt her nipples pucker.

It was dark, but she could swear she saw an answering bulge inside Emon's black pants. Or maybe that was a shadow? It was hard to tell in the dark.

He cleared his throat. "Are you looking at my dick?"

"What? Me? No."

Her eyes shot up to his face. Which looked sexy and mysterious in the moonlight. Except for the smirk at the corner of his mouth.

"In case you were wondering, that *is* a boner. In my pants. Want to see it?"

She did want. She was feeling crazy and night-wild, and she wanted to wrap him around her and feel his heat, feel him hot and wild inside her, driving her to the edge.

But she wanted to hear about her wolf even more.

"Not right now, if you don't mind." Another breeze came by, making her shiver. "You know, if you were a gentleman you'd have offered me your shirt. Because it's cold."

"You know I can do better than that."

He moved toward her and put his hands on her shoulders. They were warm and strong, and just that one touch sent the warmth pulsing all the way through her. Her nipples ached, and her sex, and she felt the fire in the middle of her chest.

He bent his head and brushed his lips ever so lightly across hers. Then an energy radiated from his hands, and she was suddenly dressed.

All in black—black long-sleeved t-shirt, black jacket, black jeans. Probably black underwear—it felt like silk.

"I still can't get over how you can just, you know. Abracadabra clothes for whoever you're touching." She snapped her fingers.

"Dragon magic. Don't ask me how we ended up

with that particular ability, because I have no fucking idea."

That had been her next question, but clearly no answer.

Trish looked down at herself. "Why black?" she asked. "To match you? Because that would be semi-adorable, in a serial-killer-couple kind of way."

He laughed, then shrugged. "To fit in with the night," he said. He paused, and added, "And your wolf would like it."

"You talked to my wolf?"

He nodded. "We went for a run. I mean, she ran and I flew, but we were together."

Trish was so stunned she had to sit down. "She didn't attack you? She actually decided it would be fun to hang out and not bite you to death?"

"Well...I was flying. So her teeth couldn't reach me." Emon sat down next to her. "Plus, you know. Dragon hide? So no. Although she did threaten to kill me," he added. "It was cute."

"Cute." She-Wolf attacked everyone. She was a killer. And Emon was calling her 'cute'.

"Yeah. She and my dragon kind of hit it off, actually, in a murdery we-hate-everyone sort of way."

Trish could not even.

Emon went on, "But she's black, and she loves the night. So I dressed you for her. Except for the shoes. Those are all you."

The shoes? Trish extended one leg, and her heart mooshed a little.

He'd given her glitter sneakers.

Sunset colors, she thought, though it was hard to see in the moonlight. Swirls of red and orange and gold and maybe hints of purple around the edges.

"Thanks," she said, trying to ignore her sudden teariness. "These are cool. Do I get to keep them, or do they disappear in a puff of smoke after I take them off?"

"No, they're real," he said. "You can keep them."

She leaned over and kissed his cheek. "You rock. As a boyfriend. And a stylist. And a homicidal wolf wrangler."

He looked startled, then pleased. "Here," he said. "Come to the edge."

Emon turned and dangled his feet off the edge of the cliff. After a second, Trish scooted forward next to him. It was a long way down, especially if you couldn't fly. But the heat of his body was comforting, and she knew if she ever fell, he'd fly down and catch her.

Emon rested his shoulder against hers. "Look," he said softly. "Look at the night."

Trish leaned against him, and instead of looking down, she looked up.

The moon was huge and round, with a strange blue cast to it that reminded her she wasn't on Earth anymore.

And beyond its brightness, the whole sky was once more full of stars. Galaxies with faint washes of color, and constellations that were no longer strange, because Emon had told her their stories.

A sparkly, glittery tapestry that came out every

night while the world slept.

Below that was the valley, mostly different shades of dark, but she began to see patterns. Forests and a river, and open land with warm glowing lights here and there. Farms, and a village maybe.

Lots of people all snug in their beds, while their nightmare dragon kept watch.

And tonight, a nightmare wolf.

A feeling of peace stole through Trish, something she hadn't felt since she was a little girl snuggled up in her dad's arms. Like the night was a safe and beautiful place, where she would never be alone, and nothing would ever hurt her.

As if he sensed her feelings, Emon reached over and hooked his fingers around hers, drawing her hand to his lips and pressing a kiss on her knuckles.

"Welcome to my world, Nightmare Wolf."

They sat there for a long time, until Trish finally got up the courage to ask the question that was burning in her mind.

CHAPTER 26

"What's she like? Did she talk to you at all?"

Emon still couldn't wrap his head around the fact that she and Layla had no communication at all.

His dragon was an asshole killer, but at least he was still talking to Emon. They hadn't given up on each other.

It must be so lonely.

He tightened his hand around hers and stroked the back of it gently with his fingers.

He thought carefully about what to say.

"She's angry," he said finally. "Because you didn't let her out for so long. She's a warrior, and she thinks you don't appreciate her strength, that you're ashamed of her. And so she likes to take control."

"Yeah. I figured that, from the forced Changes and the always killing of things."

"And if you must know, she's kind of full of herself."

Trish laughed. "So she doesn't need glittery purple sneakers for confidence?"

"Is that what the purple ones are for?"

"Uh huh."

He squeezed her hand. "Then that would be a no. She does not lack confidence. I told you, she was ready to take on my dragon."

"So...brave but delusional."

"Something like that."

Emon was silent for a moment. He didn't want to sound judgy, but he hated the idea of things in cages. And Trish *had* kept her wolf caged up.

"Why wouldn't you let her out?" he asked finally.

He felt Trish go quiet next to him, and he waited, still stroking her hand.

"It was when we lost our pack," she said finally, her words dropping into the night. "Years ago. We had a different pack, in a different place, and Jace's father was the alpha."

Jace Monroe. The alpha of Silverlake.

"His mate—Jace's mother—got involved with a wolf from another pack." Emon flinched. He didn't know wolves very well, but he knew enough to know what a betrayal that was.

"I don't know if the other wolf really cared about her, or was just using her, but their pack attacked ours. We had prime territory, forest and mountains..." A small, sad smile crossed her face. "It was beautiful. This reminds me of it."

She gestured with her free hand to the far mountains.

"Jace's dad waited too long to raise the territory defenses, because his mate was outside. He didn't realize...not until too late."

She went quiet for a moment, taking a deep breath. "Our pack was destroyed. Most of the adults were killed in the fighting. Jace and Rafe and Jesse escaped, and Kane. And me."

Her voice dropped. "My wolf wanted to fight. But I was so scared—wolves were getting killed all around me. I forced my wolf inside and I climbed the highest tree I could find, and I stayed up there until the fight was over, and night fell.

"In the middle of the night I finally climbed down. I still wouldn't let my wolf out, because I knew my scent would be stronger if I went wolf. I tried to find someone—anyone—but my pack was all gone. Dead, or escaped. No one knew I was still alive. I was all alone."

Her voice was shaking. Emon put his arm around her shoulders, trying to calm her shivering. "How old were you?"

"Fourteen."

He nodded. What could he say? He knew what she must have felt. The disbelief, the terror. He had been much younger, but he could still remember those feelings.

Every person who cared about you, gone. Your home, your history, everything that made you feel safe.

He'd had Mayah, though, and Ragnor the Evil Bastard, who had at least fed and clothed and educated them, and given them a safe place to live. Safe-ish. Until he totally lost it and started torturing them, but that didn't happen until they were older.

Trish had had no one.

"So what happened then?" he asked. She was still shivering. He tried to will some of his dragonfire into her.

"I sneaked back to our main compound, where the cabins were. The ones that hadn't been burned were full of wolves from the rival pack. Men, mostly. Warriors. Scary. They were talking about scouring the woods, making sure all our warriors were dead. They were hoping to find some stray females, though." She swallowed hard. "They almost caught me."

Emon rubbed her back gently, like he'd always done for Mayah when she was remembering.

"You don't have to talk about it anymore."

She shook her head. "I do. I think I have to. I don't talk to anyone and She-Wolf just gets angrier and angrier. Maybe if I tell you…"

"Okay," he said. "You tell me, and I'll hold the memory with you."

She gave a little choking sound. He didn't know if it was a laugh or a sob. Then she took a deep, shuddering breath.

She was brave, no matter what she thought.

"I stayed in human form. I'd always had trouble with my Changes, and with my wolf. I was quiet, and she was wild. But I was so terrified, and I thought the only thing that would save me was to hide among the humans. So I locked She-Wolf deep inside me, and I made my way to a populated area and let humans find me."

She took a deep breath. "I wouldn't tell them where

I came from, just that my parents were dead. Finally, they put me in foster care."

"What's that?"

"Oh." It took her a couple of seconds to realize he had no clue what humans did in her world. "It's a human thing—their government has a program where if kids lose their parents, they give them to other couples who agree to take them."

"That sounds okay."

She shrugged. "Sometimes it is. Sometimes, though, the foster parents are just in it for the money the government gives them. It's supposed to go to taking care of the kids, but…"

But not always. Because some people sucked.

"How was it for you?"

She grimaced. "Not as bad as for some others. I still had my shifter strength, so I didn't get bullied or abused like some other kids did. But…no one really cared about me, either. After being in a pack, it was…horrible. And I had to lock She-Wolf down and never let her out, or the humans might find out what I was. After a couple of years I ran away but I was still too scared to look for a wolf pack, so I ended up with a group of cat shifters. Needless to say, they weren't very fond of She-Wolf either. I had to Change on my own, and she was so out of control that eventually they asked me to leave.

"But one of them taught me to be a healer. And I was good at it. Maybe because She-Wolf was a killer."

"Like, it's some kind of a balance? She kills, and you heal?"

Trish shrugged. "Maybe."

Emon thought of Layla's words. How healing made Trish weak, and killing made Layla strong.

How they were both afraid to be like the other.

"What's wrong with killing things? Within reason, I mean. Wolves are hunters."

Trish shook her head. "If she'd stick to prey, that would be okay. But the thing is, shifter wolves are tempered by their human side. Their humans can make rational decisions, teach them the benefits of being in a good, stable pack. Help them stick to the rules of the shifter world, so that they can survive."

"But Layla won't listen to you."

Trish pulled back, staring at him. "Layla? She named herself?" Tears filled her eyes, and she looked away.

Emon reached over and put his fingers under her chin, gently turning her to face him. "Hey," he said. "Why does that make you sad?"

"It's just..." A couple of tears slipped down her face. "I made her feel like she wasn't a part of me. And now she's all alone."

"Not anymore." He kissed the tears away, one by one. "I'm her friend. And so is my dragon. They're going to be serial killers together, remember?"

She laughed through her tears. "Why does that thought make me happy? It should terrify me, but somehow I like the idea of the two of them as a crime duo."

"What about the two of us?"

She took a sharp breath, as if surprised, and then smiled. "I thought we were the sex dungeon duo."

Emon laughed. "That thought should terrify me, but somehow it makes me happy."

She wrapped her arms around his neck. "Really? How happy? Like, boner-happy?"

"Definitely."

He took her hand and put it on his crotch, where his dick had woken up and gotten inter-ested when it heard the words 'sex dungeon.' "That's total happiness, right there."

Trish rose up and straddled his thighs, facing him. She put his hand on her chest, over her heart. "Right here," she whispered, and leaned in and pressed her lips to his.

And he was inside her heart. All the feelings that had descended on him last night, that he'd tried to escape and shove away—here they all were. She'd been keeping them for him, holding them safe. All his feelings and all of hers—her sadness, and her pain, her loneliness and her hope.

That maybe someday someone would love her, and she'd feel whole.

He cupped the back of her neck with one hand and wrapped the other around her waist, deepening the kiss, trying to talk without words.

I'm here for you. As long as I'm around, my home is your safe place.

She gave a little sigh and parted her lips, giving him all of her sweetness and fire. And her hope. The crack in his heart stayed open. She'd broken him, but somehow, this time, it didn't hurt.

CHAPTER 27

It seemed like the kiss lasted forever, a moment outside of time. That fiery place in the middle of Trish's chest grew and expanded, like the sun coming up and warming the earth, chasing away the darkness.

And for that moment, she didn't feel broken, or split in two, or inadequate, or lonely.

She felt perfect.

Emon ran his fingers through her hair, wrapping it around his fist. "I love your hair," he murmured. "It was the very first thing I noticed about you. The night of the storm."

She pulled back, resting her arms on his shoulders. "You saw me in the storm?"

"Yeah." He let the hair drop down her back, smoothing it carefully. "I looked down, and there you were in the courtyard. Shining like a star, with your hair catching the light." He kissed her lips, and her cheekbone, and the side of her neck. "I already kind of knew I was done for, right then. My dragon and I were pretty much obsessed with you."

"Really." That pleased her. "So you came right inside and offered me your sex dungeon."

"Never let it be said I don't know how to impress a woman." He slid his hands around her waist, under her shirt. "Are you still cold?"

"No." She was warm, hot, melting where their bodies touched.

"Good." And then her shirt was gone, and he was ravishing her body, just with his mouth and hands. He seemed to love to kiss her, kiss her everywhere, setting tiny flames running along her skin and tasting the hollows of her neck with his tongue.

Then he pulled her hips tighter against him, pressing his hard swollen shaft against her sweet spot through her pants, rolling his hips to send waves of pleasure through her core.

He ducked his head to kiss her breasts, lifting them one after the other in his hand to tease her nipples with his teeth and his tongue.

All her nerve endings were on fire, and she needed his skin, needed nothing between them. She grabbed the neck of his t-shirt and ripped it right off him. She felt him smile, his lips against the hollow of her shoulder.

"Bad wolf," he murmured. "I sure do love me some bad wolf."

He loved her.

Trish wrapped her arms around his neck, pressing against him skin to skin, feeling the fire building inside both of them. "I sure do love me some serial-killer dragon."

He captured her lips, a deep hard kiss, claiming her with lips and tongue, biting softly at her lower lip before kissing her deeply again. He held her to him so hard she felt like he was trying to fit inside her skin, touch all of her.

She wanted all of him.

"I want you naked," she whispered against his ear. "Make me naked."

In a moment their pants were gone, his cock pressed tightly against her bare clit. Trish moaned. She was already wet and slick, and the feeling of his shaft moving up and down between her legs was making her crazy.

"You're the light in my darkness," he said softly. "Bright stars and colored galaxies. I want to fuck you so bad, wrap you around me and let you set me on fire. I want to feel you come when I'm inside you, over and over until you can't remember anything but how we are together."

Her insides completely melted.

He lifted her up until the tip of his cock was just outside her entrance. Then slowly, slowly, he let her sink down until she was completely filled with him. Hot and hard, stretching her and reaching deep inside, where no one else had ever touched.

Inside her body, inside her soul.

He gave a soft sigh, as if something released inside him, and closed his eyes. A long, slow rumble began in his chest, and she smiled. His dragon was happy.

Slowly, she raised herself and lowered down again, stroking him, and he moved his hips in rhythm, stroking her in return, both of them unable to feel anything but the place where they joined, the waves of sensation pulsing through them.

Emon leaned Trish backward, out over the abyss below, thrusting harder into her, bringing her closer to the edge. She felt the dark emptiness beneath her, only Emon's strong hand between her and the steep drop into nothing.

And it was enough. It was all she needed.

She threw her head back, leaning into his strength, knowing he would never let her fall. Overhead the stars pulsed, gods and goddesses chasing each other through the night sky, searching for happy endings to all their stories.

A tide of sensation rolled up her spine, wave after wave. Emon reached down and stroked her clit, until the wave broke and she clenched around his shaft, shuddering with the force of her orgasm.

Emon took her breast in his mouth, sucking on the super-sensitive nipple. It sent another wave of orgasms through her, and she cried out.

Emon slowed his thrusts, rocking against her, letting her catch her breath. He still sucked on her breasts, first one and then the other, and the sensations began building again.

Trish held on to Emon. He was the only solid thing in a world that had become nothing but feelings, storms of pleasure like she'd never felt before. All she could do was ride the lightning, let it take her.

His hand still moved between her legs, feather-light strokes on her clit that sent electricity rocketing up her spine. It was almost too much, and she dug her fingernails into Emon's shoulders.

Emon gave a strangled moan, his breath coming faster, his eyes glowing green in the darkness. His thrusts became harder, less controlled, and she stretched her thighs apart, trying to take him deeper still.

His thumb rubbed her clit with every stroke of his hips. "Fuck," she whispered. "I can't—"

She couldn't stand it, but she wanted more. She wanted him to rip her apart and put her back together, lose himself in her so hard neither one of them would ever find their way back unless they were together.

Emon gave one final thrust and wrapped his arm around her hips, holding her against him as he pulsed inside her, filling her with his essence, his soul, his love.

She buried her face in his neck, dissolving in one final shattering orgasm, knowing that he would always have a piece of her, that she would never be whole without him.

And it was good.

Blue lightning played around their bodies, weaving them together, welding pieces of each of their hearts and souls to the other.

She waited for his dragon to push back, push away, but she felt no resistance. Only wonder.

CHAPTER 28

They sat there for a long time, not talking, not moving. Just holding each other. And then a ray of light caught her, lighting both of them with a red-gold glow.

She turned, and gasped. The sun was coming up, the sky filling with color. Red, orange, gold, with a hint of purple.

It was amazing. They sat for a few more minutes, drinking it in, and then Emon reluctantly pulled away from her, planting one last kiss on her shoulder. "It's morning," he said. "We should be getting back."

Trish climbed slowly to her feet, hating the few inches of air between them. Her legs felt rubbery after their intense lovemaking; she wasn't even sure she could walk.

Good dragon.

"Ten miles, you said?" she asked. "Do you think I could have those clothes back? And how comfortable are these to walk in?" She held out her foot, still wearing the glitter sneakers he'd made for her. He'd left those when he disappeared everything else.

"Yes to the clothes," he said, conjuring more. This time he gave her a blue shirt, to match her eyes. "As far as the walking, no need. I hope."

<You mean me, I suppose> his dragon said. <Take the wolves here. Take the wolves there. At least Layla has the decency to run on her own four feet.>

Emon sighed.

"What?" Trish asked.

"My dragon is an asshole."

"At least he talks to you."

He heard the bitterness in her voice. He wished he could convince his dragon to persuade Layla to talk to Trish. Open up some kind of communication.

<I do not tell her what to do. No one tells her what to do.>

No shit.

Will you carry Trish back to the castle or not?

Dramatic dragon sigh. <I suppose.>

Stand back," Emon said. "And don't get near the teeth. Just in case."

Trish backed away, and Emon Changed. He knew what he looked like. Huge, black as night, deadly barbs all over his body. Some of them held venom chambers that injected poison into whatever they penetrated.

His dragon let out a huge roar, and breathed lightning into the air above them. Then he waited to see what Trish would do.

Brock hadn't been scared of him, but Brock was, well…Brock. He was six years old and he trusted everyone.

Steeling himself, Emon looked at Trish, who was staring at him. Not in terror—not even with awe.

With delight. And amazement.

"Wow," she murmured. "I've never seen you in the sunlight before. You are...breathtaking. So beautiful."

Beautiful?

<Beautiful?> his dragon echoed. <*She means terrifying. I am terrifying.*> But he sounded uncertain. He lowered his head toward Trish, as if he wanted to get a better look at her.

No biting, Emon said. *Please.*

<Layla is inside her. I like Layla.>

Trish was walking around him, still staring. "The sunrise reflects off your scales. Red and orange and purple. I've never seen anything so gorgeous."

Tentatively, he reached out with his mind, to see if he could see what she was seeing.

With shocking swiftness, a full picture jumped from her mind to his. A black dragon on a cliff, shimmering with the colors of the sunrise: a creature of glittering, awesome beauty.

That's how she saw him. His dragon was stunned into silence.

"Can I touch you?" she asked softly.

He crouched down almost without realizing he was doing it, and extended his neck a bit further, so that his head was just a foot away from her. Everything in him yearned for her touch.

She reached out a hand and gently brushed it across his nose, tracing the bony ridges over his nostrils. Then she walked along beside his giant head, trailing her fingers over his scaly skin.

"These tiny scales are so soft!" She ran her fingers

across his eye ridge, caressing it. His eyelids dropped half-shut, and he suddenly had the urge to purr.

Trish ran her hand down the length of his neck, walking next to him, and stroked his furled wing. "A dragon," she said, her voice full of wonder. "It's like magic."

I am magic, he said, forgetting she couldn't hear him.

Her eyes got huge. "You can talk in my head!"

You heard that?

"Wasn't I supposed to?"

I didn't think you would. Most people can't hear us. Brock can, with his abilities. And Layla can. That's how I knew her name.

And I can. She walked up and stroked his eye ridge again, looking pleased.

Emon said, *I'm going to pick you up now, so we can fly.* He sat up and grasped her carefully with one of his foreclaws, making sure he didn't cut her with his talons. He set her in the palm of his other foreclaw, cupping it slightly to make a comfortable place for her to sit. Then he loosened the hand that held her, but kept it wrapped around so that it encircled her like a safety cage.

Hold on. And he jumped off the cliff.

He felt Trish gasp as they plunged toward the valley below. Then he snapped his wings out and glided across the valley before he beat them powerfully, lifting them into the air.

Trish let her breath out in a loud whoop. "Oh my god, this is amazing!"

She climbed to her knees, peering out over the talons

that held her safe. "It's like the best amusement park ride ever!"

What's an amusement park?

"Never mind. This is better."

Trish's mind was freaking blown. Traveling by dragon was by far the most amazing thing she'd ever done. She could see the ground below them like a tapestry, a hundred shades of green and brown. In the distance was the castle, dark and brooding, amidst its emerald green fields dotted with sheep.

She put her cheek against Emon's front foot. It had fingers, like a lizard foot, covered in the same teeny-tiny scales as his head, so supple and warm they felt like the softest of skin. She wanted to pet him like a cat. She didn't know how his dragon would feel about that, though he'd seemed to like it when she was touching him before.

Maybe he wasn't such a terrifying monster after all. Maybe he was just lonely, and starved for love. Maybe he and Emon both were. She knew Mayah loved him, but Emon had always taken care of her. He'd never had someone to take care of him.

They landed on the huge flat roof of the castle. Trish almost didn't want to get out of his arms. She had the wild urge to just fly off with him, into the mountains, into the sunrise, and leave everything else behind.

Except the darkness—Layla—would still be with her.

But Emon had seen her darkness, seen the killer wolf that lived inside her, and he still wanted her.

He was a dragon—the one person she couldn't hurt, who Layla couldn't destroy.

Hell, he even liked her.

Trish suddenly wished she could talk to Layla. See what it was the dragon liked—assuming it was something other than her murderiness.

But she wasn't going to think about that now. She was going to think about sunrises and kisses and glitter sneakers.

She climbed down. "Thank you for the beautiful flight," she said.

<*I suppose it wasn't totally heinous*> said a dry, grumpy voice in her mind.

Oh my god. The dragon was talking to her.

<*But I like you better as a wolf.*>

He suddenly reminded her of Kane, their Enforcer. Who pretended he hated everyone, but on the inside, wanted nothing more desperately than to belong.

"Nah, you love us both," she said. "Especially glittery me." She held out her foot.

<*Don't hold out treats for me unless you really mean it.*>

"If you try to eat me I'll rub your eye ridges and kiss you on the nose until you roll over and purr like a kitten."

<*In your dreams, human.*>

But his eyelids dipped a little, as if he were thinking about getting his eye ridges rubbed. Holding her breath, Trish leaned over and really did kiss his nose.

His eyes snapped open. Trish held her breath.

Crap, he's going to eat me, she thought.

Instead, he gave a disgusted snort, enveloping her in smoke. There was a momentary roar of wind like a giant vacuum cleaner, and then the dragon was gone and Emon was standing in front of her.

"Well," he said. "That didn't go as badly as I thought it might."

"Me either," she said. "He didn't even singe me with that last snort." He could have burned her like a torch.

"I can't believe you kissed him."

"Why not? It worked. It turned him into a prince."

Emon laughed. "Not sure the prince is a better bargain."

"He has his moments." She put her arms around his neck, and he kissed her—hot, then warm and sweet, then gentle and tender.

They gazed into each other's eyes for a long moment, both their hearts too full for words.

Then Emon said, "Oh, I forgot to tell you. I did a restoration spell on the clothes you were wearing the other night. When you Changed. I wouldn't have wanted you to be without your purple confidence sneakers."

He'd remembered they were her favorites. And he'd fixed them for her, even after she'd bitten him. Tears prickled her eyes. "I can't believe you did that. Thank you."

She held out her foot. "But I have a new favorite pair now."

A smile flashed at the corner of his mouth and was gone. But it didn't matter whether she saw the smiles or not.

She knew his secret now. These weren't sunset colors at all. They were sunrise colors. Because deep down inside, he believed that the world wasn't only darkness.

Eventually, if you were patient enough, the sun would come up.

CHAPTER 29

The following day, Emon came and found Trish in the lab around lunchtime. The other researchers eyed him warily as he clomped through in his heavy boots, still dressed all in black, looking like the Draken version of a biker gang leader.

Their mouths dropped open as he grabbed her, bent her backwards, and planted a toe-curling, panty-melting kiss on her.

"Trish is taking the afternoon off," he said. "Don't wait up."

He swept her up and carried her out of the lab. There was a scattering of applause.

"Ooh, don't tell me," Trish said when they got out into the hallway. "You finally finished the sex dungeon."

"Stop it. You know the words 'sex dungeon' always give me a boner. And no. I've been busy."

"Well then, your unrequited boner is your own fault. If not the sex dungeon, then what?"

"I want to show you something. And then I'm taking you on a field trip, if you want."

"I love field trips. Are you going to show me your

boner first?"

"I think if we get into boner show and tell, the field trip has a 99% chance of not happening. So no. Maybe after, if you're a good little wolf."

"Hah. I think I have more chance of getting my hands on the boner if I'm a big bad wolf."

"Probably."

Emon carried her through the castle, to a corridor on the fourth floor she'd never been to. "These are my official rooms," he said, pushing the door open. "Which I don't use. But I could, if you like them."

It was a suite, with a bedroom similar to hers, only even bigger and more ostentatious, and with even more bloody battle scenes decorating the walls. *And* an even more fantastic bathroom, and a way-too-formal sitting room.

"I was thinking I could replace the furniture in here with something more comfortable, get another generator so we can have a TV and computers, and a fridge so there's cold beer."

Trish's mouth fell open. "Are you asking me to move in with you?"

He dropped his eyes, rubbing the back of the sofa with one hand. "I guess, yeah." He raised his eyes to hers. "Would you? I mean, I don't know if I can sleep inside in a bed, but I could try. And even if I can't, this could be our place to hang out."

Trish flung her arms around his neck. "Yes. I'd love to live with you. On one condition."

"Oh, shit. I hate conditions. What?"

"Can we find different tapestries for the walls?"

Emon laughed. "I thought Layla would like all the blood and death."

"She probably does. But I'm not so in love with it. Maybe we could compromise? Blood and death in here, and something a little more peaceful in the bedroom?"

"Done." He kissed her nose. "Now come in the study. This is what I really want to show you."

The study was exactly what you'd expect—walls of built-ins, leather-bound books, a big manly desk and a comfortable-looking leather chair and sofa for reading. Emon went over to the bookcase to the right of the fireplace, moving one of the books and pressing his thumb to a certain spot on the wall behind it.

The whole bookcase moved, revealing a secret room.

Okay, that was fucking awesome. "A secret bookcase door! Just like one of my books. I've always wanted one of these. Is there a nun from like, a hundred years ago, walled up inside?"

"First, I don't know what a nun is, so probably not. And second, those books are weird and disturbing."

"I know. So what's in here, if it's not a nun skeleton?"

"You'll see."

She walked in and gasped. The whole room was filled with beautiful objects made from that purplish metal she'd seen in the drawing room, and a few other places in the castle.

Jewelry on display stands, small statues and ornaments, pieces that looked like magical artifacts, engraved with runes and sigils.

They all radiated energy, as if the room was humming just below her threshold of hearing.

"Wow," was all Trish could manage to say. "This is…incredible."

"It's all made from atherias. It's one of the most valuable metals in all the worlds—holds magical power better than gold." He took a deep breath and then said, "It's my hoard."

Trish looked around, stunned. A dragon's hoard was his most precious, most private thing. They didn't show them to just anyone. Most of them didn't show them to anyone at all.

She reached up and kissed him softly. "I'm honored," she said. He smiled—one of his few true smiles that made his eyes light up, and made him look suddenly young and hopeful.

"I have to go out to the mine this afternoon, and I thought—I was hoping—you might want to go with me. I wanted you to see what it is before we went. And to give you something."

He went to a small cabinet on one wall and opened a drawer, coming out with a rough purple rock about the size of a tennis ball. "This is what atherias looks like in its raw form."

He put the rock on his palm, held it in front of him, closed his eyes…and began to sing.

The sound started low, and then slowly grew until it seemed to fill the whole room, every cell of her body, every beat of her heart. There were words, but in a language she didn't understand—and yet she did. Longing. Desire. Hope. Love.

Slowly, as he sang, the lump of rock changed shape. Rough, at first, but then she saw four protrusions becoming legs, and paws. A feathery tail, lifted high. A head with a muzzle and pointed ears, raised in pride and defiance.

A wolf.

The statue grew in detail and expression, until Trish almost expected it to come to life and run right off Emon's hand. And then the song rose to a crescendo, and ended.

Emon opened his eyes, looked at the wolf, and smiled. Then he held it out to her. "Here. This is for you. It's Layla."

Tears spilled down Trish's cheeks. "She's beautiful."

Emon caught the tears with his thumb, wiping them away. "Yeah. She is. And I wanted you to have this, so you can look at it and see her the way I see her."

Trish took the wolf, cradling it in her hand. This was a gift from his hoard, and from his heart. The most precious thing her dark dragon could give her.

She wrapped her other arm around his waist, leaning her head on his chest. "Thank you," she whispered. For much more than the gift. For giving her a part of himself.

Emon cleared his throat. "So, you want to see the mine?" he said. "It's not far—not if we fly there. And I have to check on the production and talk to the miners."

"I'd love to," Trish said.

"Great." He looked pleased. "Only, fair warning. The Wild Dragons who mine it are a fucking pain in my ass, and they used to work for Ragnor. They shouldn't be dangerous, because they know I'll fucking kill them if they try anything, but just because I'm paranoid, stay where I can see you. And watch yourself."

"Yes, my prince." She saluted.

Emon shook his head, muttering something about Mayah's influence and women who had no respect.

Trish kissed him on the shoulder and put her wolf on the shelf for safekeeping, before following him up to the roof.

CHAPTER 30

The flight to the mine was no less fantastic than the flight the other morning. "This is never going to get old," Trish said happily, snuggled into the palm of Emon's giant dragony hand.

<I should hope not> his dragon said. <If you were to start taking us for granted already, I might have to squash you.>

Trish kissed one of his huge fingers, where it wrapped around to keep her from falling, and he gave a pleased little grumble.

The mine was on the side of one of the tallest mountains that ringed the perimeter of Emon's domain. From the air, she could see it was mostly bare rock and dirt, with a few scrubby trees here and there.

It was easy to see where the mine was—a vast dark cave entrance surrounded by a fence that glowed faintly blue with magic. At one side, in a sheltered nook, she saw a rough camp surrounded by smaller caves, still big enough for a dragon to sleep in.

"Are the Wild Dragons stuck in there?" she asked Emon. "Inside the fence."

No, he said shortly. *I don't cage people—even criminals.*

And they have to be able to get out, to hunt for food.

She rested her cheek against his hand for a moment.

"Then, do you think it's them that have been killing the sheep? And breaking into Ragnor's study?"

Whoever it was, they were cloaked like a dragon. It's the only explanation for why you couldn't hear them, or scent them.

"But what would they want with Ragnor's research?"

Sell it? Emon said. They were circling down now, to land in front of the mine. *They're magically bound here to this domain, as part of their punishment, but a powerful enough Draken or sorcerer could break that. They might want the research to buy their way out—and to find out how to make a portal to contact an outsider.*

"You'd think they'd just steal some atherias and buy their way out, if it's that valuable. Instead of risking themselves breaking into the castle."

Depends who they're dealing with. If it's Gen-X, they might not have a use for atherias. They'd want the research.

Gen-X. Just the thought made Trish's stomach curdle—they'd tried to kidnap Tristan and Brock not so long ago, along with Tristan's sister Terin. "I hope it's not them."

I don't know if I hope it is or it isn't, Emon said. *At least I'd know who I was dealing with. If it's not them, then who the fuck is it?*

Trish had no answer to that.

They landed in front of the entrance to the mine, Emon Changing back to human. Trish was about to ask where the dragons were, when she heard them.

Singing.

Deep inside the mine, they were singing the ore out of the mountain. As amazing as Emon's song had been when he made her wolf for her, this was...she had no words.

It wasn't just beautiful. It hit her deep in her soul. It was a song to coax the very earth to give up its treasures into the dragons' keeping. A love song, a song of praise. A song of joy.

The joy flowed out of the song and into her. At the same time, she and Emon reached for each other's hands and held on. He just stood, listening, a small contented smile on his face.

After she didn't know how long, the song faded away. Emon picked up a curved horn hanging from a protrusion in the rock, and blew a long note to summon the dragons out.

Trish waited, unable to believe that people who could create a song like that—audible joy—could be evil traitors working with Gen-X.

That was before she met Zakerek.

The Wild Dragon was tall, almost as tall as Emon, with a golden blond mohawk and tattoos on the shaved parts of his scalp.

And a really bad attitude.

"Your Exalted Highness," he said, giving an exaggerated bow. The other two dragons gave small, jerky, obviously reluctant bows of their own. They were all dressed in boots and work pants, no shirts.

Damn. Dragons really were the hottest shifters anywhere. And Trish lived with a pack of wolves that were drop-dead gorgeous.

Zakerek went on, "What brings you to grace our poor, insignificant selves with your presence today?"

His tone was sarcastic and his eyes were resentful—dark and angry, with red flames dancing in the pupils.

"The monthly reports are late, and so is the ore shipment," Emon said. "Also, more sheep have gone missing, and someone has been lurking around the castle. Cloaked. Do you know anything about that, by some chance?"

The other two dragons shuffled back and forth and exchanged glances, but Zakerek just stared defiantly at Emon. "What if we did?" he said. "You're clearly not smart enough to catch us. So maybe you're not smart enough to rule over us, either. I know you can't imagine us finding any place nicer than here—" he waved his hand expansively at the desolate land, and the rough camp beyond— "but you'd be shocked to learn that other people besides yourself enjoy fine meals and exotic entertainment."

He fixed his eyes on Trish, insolently looking her up and down. Emon growled, and the other two dragons looked uncomfortable.

Emon gazed from one to the other of them, eyes narrowed. Then he looked directly at one of the other dragons. "Cazbek, did you take my sheep or sneak into my castle?"

The dragon looked startled, then wary. "No, your

highness."

He fixed his eyes on the other one. "Mikah, did you take my sheep or sneak into my castle?"

"No, your highness." He didn't meet Emon's eyes, but Trish, at least, couldn't hear a lie in his voice.

Emon said, "Zakerek, a word with you in private."

He walked Zakerek off to one side, leaving Trish with the other two dragons, who looked even more uncomfortable now—though not as uncomfortable as she felt.

Cazbek said, "You're one of those wolves, aren't you. The ones with mind powers. Stay out of my head." Before she could explain that she *wasn't* the one with the mind powers, he stalked off to a barrel of water standing by the mine entrance and started sluicing himself down, washing some of the dirt off his chest. Even though Trish's heart belonged to Emon, she had trouble tearing her gaze away.

Mikah was watching her, amusement on his face. He came over to stand next to her. Trish watched him warily, but Emon was within shouting distance, having a low-voiced argument with Zakerek.

"I'm Mikah," he said, holding out his hand.

Trish shook it. "I'm Trish." She almost said, "Of the Silverlake pack," but realized she didn't know if that was quite true anymore. Officially, Jace hadn't released her from the pack, but she belonged with Emon.

"You're that wolf that Emon's been—" He trailed off, maybe realizing that 'fucking' or 'boinking' or 'fantasizing about sex dungeons with' weren't exactly appropriate to say, in the circumstances.

He took a deep breath, and then said, "Are you two going to mate?"

Trish was shocked—and she didn't know what to say. "Why do you care?" she asked instead.

Mikah glanced over at Zakerek, as if he wanted to make sure he wasn't listening. Cazbek *was* listening, but Mikah didn't seem to care about that.

He dropped his voice lower. "Look, I don't care what you two are doing in bed, or wherever dragons do it. But the Darkwing Dragon is fucked up. If he doesn't find a mate, he'll implode, and this whole place will go with him."

He gestured out at the view below the mountain. "He's a Draken prince, born to rule, and he's good at it, when he's not losing his shit. All that down there—it's a really nice place to live." He sounded almost wistful.

"Royal Draken don't just need a hoard," he said. "They need a purpose. If they don't have one, it eats away at them. And they need a clan. Other Draken." He turned to face her again. "If you're his mate, that's... whatever. But he still needs other Draken. And if he's forming a clan, I want in. Me and Cazbek both do." She heard a snort from over by the water barrel—but no disagreement.

"And Zakerek does too, no matter how he acts," Mikah added. "So...if you have any influence at all over the Darkwing Dragon, maybe you could put in a good word for us?"

Trish studied him, wishing she did have some of

Tristan's or Brock's mind powers. Wishing she could see if he was really a good dragon—or just a good actor.

But if Mikah was right—if royal Draken needed more than just a mate, more than a hoard, then…

An idea she'd had while working on the toxin took root in her mind.

"I'll think about it," she said slowly. Mikah nodded. "Was it really not any of you lurking around the castle?"

Mikah shrugged. "We're not together every second," he said, glancing over at Zakerek. "Who could stand that?" He paused, then added, "But there are other creatures who can cloak themselves. Sorcerers. Ki-rin. And magic artifacts can do it too. It doesn't have to be us."

Which was not helpful at all.

CHAPTER 31

Emon was quiet on the way back, and Trish didn't disturb him, just spent the short flight watching the view change as they flew.

The closer they got to the castle, though, the more she could feel his emotions churning.

"What is it?" she asked finally.

I'm not sure, he said. *Something's wrong. I feel...I'm not sure.*

As soon as his feet touched the rooftop, though, he suddenly got sure. The dragon let out a roar of rage, fire spewing from his jaws.

<Our hoard! Someone has stolen from our hoard!>

He let Trish tumble from his hands, barely bothering to see that she was standing upright. Then he Changed and headed for the stairs at a run, Trish right behind him.

Kill the thief, Layla muttered inside her. *Kill...*

Not now, Trish told her. That was the last thing she or Emon needed—Layla running amok amidst the furor. It was going to be all they could do to contain Emon's dragon.

By the time she made it to Emon's rooms, he was

already in the study, the door to the atherias room open.

Trish wasn't familiar with the contents of the room, but even she could see gaps in the shelves. She checked for the little wolf Emon had made for her, and was relieved to see it still on the shelf. She would have been devastated to lose that.

How had this happened? And why now?

At least the red dragons had been telling the truth. None of them could have done this, and since it was unlikely that there was more than one person sneaking around the castle causing trouble, that meant it probably hadn't been one of them searching Ragnor's study either.

But if not them, then who? And was this what they'd been after all along? Not the research, but the atherias? Or was it both?

Emon already had Grange on the communicator. His voice was harsh and raspy, his dragon in his eyes. "Everyone is confined to quarters until further notice," he said. "Research team included—all except Trish. She was with me. Then I want this whole castle searched, top to bottom. Magical recorders on all the searchers, to keep them honest. If anyone from outside has been in any part of the castle today, including delivering food, I want their homes and outbuildings searched as well."

"Your highness, do you really think—"

"Do it."

Trish stayed with Emon as the search team went through the castle. He had a screen in his office that collected the feeds from all the searchers' recording devices—sort of a magical security system.

They were only an hour into the search when Grange unearthed a golden box hidden in a supply crate in one of the researchers' rooms. It was a spell cage—specially created to mask and contain the magic of anything placed inside.

It held half a dozen atherias spell artifacts from Emon's hoard, as well as research notes from Ragnor's study. And a silicone finger with a replica of Emon's fingerprint, along with a vial of his blood—one that he'd trusted Trish to collect from him.

The man had used the fingerprint and blood to mimic Emon's DNA signature and open the vault.

The researcher was marched down to the portal immediately and sent back to Earth in the custody of one of Noah's security guards, protesting his innocence the whole way. Emon insisted that the rest of the research team also be sent back.

"At least let them pack," Mina said.

"No." Emon was adamant. "Their things can be sent back later, after they've been thoroughly searched. But I want them gone. For all you know, they're all working for Gen-X."

He looked around the room. Brock was sitting huddled up on one sofa, his knees to his chest, and Mina had her arm around him. Mayah was sitting on another sofa, and Tristan and Noah were pacing. Emon said, "Hell, for all I know, you all are working for them."

"Now just a damn fucking minute," Noah said,

getting up in Emon's face.

Bad idea; Emon's eyes went dragony and he hissed.

Trish put a hand on Emon's arm, trying to calm him. He was so tense it was like touching a steel bar.

Noah ignored the hiss and the dragon eyes. "Listen to me, you motherfucker. Two years ago, Gen-X almost wiped out the Bad Blood Crew, trying to capture Brock and Tristan and Terin. They nearly killed Mina—I had to Turn her to save her life. If you think for one fucking nanosecond that any of us would collude with them—for any reason—then you're a bigger idiot than I already thought you were."

Emon growled, and smoke began to come out of his nostrils.

Oh, shit.

"He's right, Emon," Mayah said softly. "I'm not saying that a traitor—or more than one—couldn't have been inserted into the research team, no matter how carefully they were vetted. Obviously one was. But no one in this room had anything to do with it. I think we should let them stay. I want them to keep treating me."

"Fine." Emon spat out the words. "But everyone else goes. I should have known better than to let strangers into our domain. They always betray us." And he stomped out of the room.

CHAPTER 32

Two nights later, Grange slipped down the stairs to the lowest dungeon. He used his magical cloaking device so no one would see him, as he'd been doing for all these months as he searched the castle, watching its inhabitants.

Learning the things he needed to fulfill his mission.

The only one who could possibly see through the spell was the Darkwing Draken, and there was no worry about running into him. He was out flying in the darkness, brooding over his betrayals and misfortunes. And if he came back, he'd head for Trish's bed.

The one who liked all those gothic romance books.

Too bad it had to be her the dragon had chosen. Grange had kind of liked her. But no one could be allowed to stand in the way of him bringing down the last of the House of Al-Maddeiri—and making sure Ragnor's research was safe from them.

In his hand he clutched the King's Key—a flat round disk of atherias, infused with the blood of Al-Maddeiri. Among other things, it gave the user the ability to open or close any portal within the bounds of the domain.

He'd been hunting for it for so long, and had finally

managed to locate it in the seldom-used safe in the prince's rooms. Stealing the atherias pieces as well had been an inspired move—the prince's dragon had been so obsessed with his hoard, he hadn't even thought to check the safe.

And now Grange could finally finish his mission. He'd planned, and schemed, drugging the princess to make her crazy—crazier—and carefully nudging the prince until he'd not only invited Tristan Barnes and Brock Reilly here, within Grange's reach, but also unlocked Ragnor's research for them.

And then Grange had managed to get the research team out of the way, planting the atherias artifacts, the blood and the fake fingerprint he'd used to get into the safe and the hoard room on one of them.

He hadn't even had to convince Emon to allow the Reillys and Tristan Barnes to stay, though. Mayah had done that for him.

Now all he had to do was get rid of Trish, and Noah Reilly. But first he had to get the Darkwing Draken out of the way for a day or two.

But Grange had a plan for that too—inside the backpack over his shoulder. Some nice, targeted explosives.

Reaching the dungeon, he used the Key to set wards around the room, to keep either of the Al-Maddeiri dragons from sensing the magic he was about to use.

Then he activated the Key, opened a portal, and walked through. He'd take care of this one last task, and be back before morning.

CHAPTER 33

Trish was up early, working in the lab. With the rest of the team gone, she'd been working even more hours trying to get a handle on the toxin and what it was doing to Emon's wound.

Everyone in the castle was upset and on edge. Trish still didn't know if she believed that the researcher really was the guilty one, but she did know that the hurt and betrayal Emon felt had made his wound worse.

He still made love to her, but the playful humor was gone, replaced by dark ferocity followed by an almost desperate tenderness.

She was just rubbing her bleary eyes when Grange appeared in the doorway, holding a coffee tray. "Hey," he said quietly. "I thought you might be able to use this."

"You are a prince among—well, among princes and princesses," she said. He set it down on the lab table and Trish poured herself a mug. "Thanks."

Even Grange had been affected by the upsets in the castle. His golden glow had dimmed, and his usually friendly and open face looked wary. "How's the prince?" he asked.

Trish waggled her hand in a 'so-so' gesture. "Not that good. He hasn't even been sleeping on the roof the last couple of nights—just spends half the night flying around in the dark. I'm worried about him, to tell you the truth."

Grange nodded. "Me too. I'd hoped being with you would help mitigate his Al-Maddeiri instability, but..." He let the words trail off.

Trish wanted to punch him in his friendly innocent face. Emon was *not* going to slide off into insanity, just because something in his life had gone wrong. "He'll be okay," she said. "It will just take a little time."

Grange gave a little shrug, like Emon had always been a lost cause and she'd figure it out sooner or later. She wanted to punch him again, which was probably wrong of her, because he'd just brought her coffee.

Grange's communicator went off with a hollow musical sound. He glanced at Trish, then answered. "Head Steward here," he said. She could hear a soft murmuring as someone on the other end talked to him.

Trish went back to her tests. The sooner she could figure out how to counteract this damn toxin, the sooner she could prove Grange wrong.

Emon had been out most of the night, flying. He knew Trish hated it when he left her in the middle of the night, but he couldn't sleep. All that rage and helplessness and betrayal just sloshed around inside him, eating him up from inside.

It was a race to see which would devour him first—

the inner wound or the outer one. Somehow even being with Trish didn't make it better anymore.

<We should bite her and claim her like the wolves do> his dragon said. <So she won't leave us.>

Cage her, you mean? She'd be better off without us.

<You said she would heal us. Maybe if we claimed her, she would.>

Fucking dreamer. Which was a thing he'd never though he'd say about his dragon.

Trish wasn't in their rooms, so he headed for the lab. Grange was there, just finishing a call on his communicator when Emon arrived.

"Thank goodness you're here, your Highness. I just got a call from the iron mines out at the eastern edge of the territory," Grange said. "There was a major rock slide. Some kind of earth tremor collapsed part of the mine, and blocked off the main road access. It sounds pretty bad."

Fuck. He could have sworn those mountains were stable. "Was anyone killed? Are there workers trapped in the mine?"

Grange shook his head. "I don't think so. It happened just an hour ago, before the daily shift started. According to the mine manager, the main problem is the rubble covering the road. They're cut off—no food, no extra supplies, no help from the neighboring communities. They're asking if you—your dragon—could come out and clear the road for them. And maybe help them dig out the mine? If they have to do it themselves, production could be halted for weeks."

<I am not a mine worker> his dragon grumbled. <Or a beast of burden. We are a King of the Draken. We do not do manual labor.>

A King of the Draken without other Draken subjects to do our dirty work, Emon said. *We're going to have to do it ourselves.*

<If I break a claw heaving rubble around, you owe me a manicure.>

Emon suppressed a smile. *Talk to Mayah about that. If you're nice, she'll probably give you one. She can paint little flowers on your claws with nail polish.*

His dragon growled.

Grange looked slightly alarmed at the growl. "Begging your pardon, but I really think you should go, Your Highness," he said. "I'm sure, with your dragon's might, it won't take more than a day or so to put things right."

Somehow that whole 'Your Highness' thing, along with Grange's subservient sucking up, turned Emon's stomach. Or maybe it was just that he hated everybody right now.

"I'm on my way," he said to Grange. "Let them know I'm coming."

Grange nodded, looking abnormally relieved, and headed out the door.

Had he really thought Emon was going to just let his people struggle through on their own? Asshole.

He turned to Trish. "Do you want to come with me? I—"

He stopped, getting a good look at her face. "Are you okay?"

She looked pale, her eyes a bit unfocused.

"I don't know," she said. "I feel kind of...sick? I'm not really sure. Shifters don't normally get sick."

He knew the feeling. With his magical Draken healing and immune system, he'd never been sick either, until his wound. The toxin...

Fuck.

Emon said, "The toxin. Is there any way it could have gotten into your system?"

Trish shook her head. "I'm always careful. And anyway, it's keyed to dragons, not wolves."

He knew that. He knew that, but he still didn't like this. "Get Tristan to check you out. Okay?"

She nodded. "Stop worrying. It's probably just Layla. Or some weird food from this world, that doesn't agree with me."

"I still don't like it. Maybe you should come with me."

"You'll be too busy to babysit me. I'll be fine. Go."

Emon hesitated, but he really was needed out at the mine. And Trish was better off without him right now.

"Promise me you'll get Tristan to check you out. And you'll call me on the communicator if you need anything."

She kissed his cheek. "I promise, worrywart."

He hugged her tightly, and then made himself leave.

After Emon and Grange left, Trish went back to her research. She kept thinking about what Mikah the red dragon had said, about royal Draken needing a purpose.

Not having one could eat away at them.

Was that what she'd missed, in this toxin? Had Ragnor somehow managed to find a toxin not just for a Draken's body, but for their soul? Intensifying Emon's feeling of hopelessness, purposelessness, and turning it into a physical wound that wouldn't heal?

Draken were magical creatures, after all. Could magically attacking the essence of who they were be just as deadly as attacking them physically?

Trish went frantically back through Ragnor's notes again, and his list of ingredients for the last versions of the toxin, the ones he'd tested on Emon.

There was one that had been in the last few versions, and she still couldn't figure out what it was or what it did. *Dahshi.*

She looked it up again in her database, and did a keyword search through the research team's notes and documents. Nothing. Then she remembered the new database, the one from Tyr Greystone, a Wild Dragon healer on Earth. They'd received it just before everything went to hell.

There it was. Dahshi. Nightmare weed. A hallucinogenic native to the Dragonlands that caused horrible nightmares and, in larger doses, induced long-term psychosis and/or suicidal depression in humans. Could also affect shifters and even Draken, when combined with certain spells or magical substances...

Fuck. Fuck, fuck, fuck. Ragnor had infused his damn toxin—infused Emon—with a despair that latched onto his soul—and was killing him from the inside out.

She looked up from the computer and was hit with a sudden bout of vertigo. Strange colors swirled around the edges of her vision.

I feel wrong, Layla was whispering. *Wrong, wrong, wrong...*

She'd been drugged, Trish realized, her mind whirling. She had to take a blood sample...get Tristan...she wasn't sure what to do first. Her gaze fell on the half-empty coffee cup sitting on the counter.

Damn. The coffee...

She reached for it, and the room lurched. She felt a sting on her shoulder, like a bug bite.

And then all the colors turned to black.

CHAPTER 34

Trish woke up surrounded by the smell of blood. In the air, in the ground below her, even on her skin.

What the hell...

Her eyes were sticky and her head was splitting. She could feel the sun on her skin, the hard-packed earth gritty underneath her.

Which meant she was naked. Which meant she'd Changed. And all the blood meant...Layla had killed. And killed, and killed...

Trish forced her eyes open and sat up. She was in some kind of animal enclosure with a high board fence around it. A sheep enclosure.

She could tell because of the strong smell of sheep. And because of all the bloody, torn, dismembered bodies around her.

She felt sick.

Layla had gone crazy and killed at least twenty of Emon's sheep. But why?

Something was wrong. She sometimes felt disoriented after a Change, but not like this.

Through her foggy haze, she heard voices. Faint, but getting closer. Grange, she realized. And Noah.

"There has to be some mistake," Noah was saying. "Trish would never do something like that."

Grange's voice was unhappy. "You may not know as much about her as you think you do," he said. "I mean, don't get me wrong. I like her too—in her human form. But..."

"What?" Noah said impatiently.

"Well, she's hiding a lot from you all. Her and the white wolf. Tristan. I mean, at first I didn't think it was any of my business." He hesitated, then went on. "But now it is. Even if she'd just attacked the sheep—but attacking me too? She tried to kill me. She's dangerous."

She'd tried to kill Grange? Fuck. How could this have happened? *Layla, what did you do?*

Trish tried to get to her feet, looking for something to cover herself with so she didn't have to face Grange and Noah naked.

"Look at these bite marks." The voices were louder now. "They're still bleeding. And these. And she got me pretty good with the claws, too."

There was blood all over her. Under her nails. On her face. In her mouth. Thank god Grange was a lion— Layla might have killed him.

Would have. He is a pussy. Layla sounded smug. *Did not attack.*

Trish ignored her, straining her ears to hear what Grange was saying. What she had to somehow defend herself against. Noah was an Enforcer. He would be acting in his official capacity, not as her friend.

And Emon was on the other side of his domain. She

wasn't officially mated to him, or released from the Silverlake pack. Noah could—would probably have to—take her into custody, back to Silverlake. To the Council.

"Something about her didn't sit right with me from the beginning," Grange was saying now. "Maybe it's easier for an outsider to see? But she can't even Change without Tristan or Emon to babysit her, make sure her wolf doesn't go on a killing spree. And she's attacked them both. She almost killed Tristan when she first got here. Practically ripped his throat out. I don't know why he's protecting her."

How did he know that? Only Emon knew, and Mayah. Had Emon told Grange? Terror began to spread cold tentacles through Trish. She couldn't ask Tristan to lie for her—he'd risk punishment from the council.

They were going to find out everything. She'd be arrested. Put in a cage. Maybe put down. How could she have let this happen? How could Layla have done it?

Did not, Layla said, more forcefully. *Told you.*

That took Trish aback. Layla always took credit for her kills, for her fights. She was proud, even defiant. Why would she deny it now?

Who the fuck did, then? she asked, not really expecting an answer.

But she got one. For the first time, Layla responded to her.

Do not know. There was a pause. *Confused. But we did not do it.*

This didn't make sense. But if they hadn't done it... Trish tried to think back, to the last thing she remembered. She'd seen Emon in the lab. He'd left for the iron mine. Then she'd...what did she do after that? It was all hazy.

Except...Her hand went to her shoulder. That stinging pain. Under her fingers was a faint indentation, barely discernable.

A nearly-healed puncture. Like from a tranquilizer dart.

She'd been set up.

Grange had set her up.

Things started coming back to her, clicking into place. The feeling of being drugged. The coffee. And now the false accusations. Grange was making it look like Layla was a dangerous killer.

I am. But I did not do this.

Grange had. But why?

She didn't have time to figure it out. Grange and Noah were almost here. And if Noah took her back to Silverlake, she wouldn't see Emon again.

She wouldn't be able to warn him that Grange was the one who had betrayed him. She had to get out of here.

She looked up, seeing a faint spell net stretched along the fencing and over the top of the enclosure. No way over or through the fence. He'd thought of everything.

I dig, Layla said.

There was no time for second-guessing herself. She let the wolf have her body.

Grange and Noah were right at the gate.

"You shouldn't have just left her out here," Noah said.

"I had to," Grange sounded defensive. "I needed you to see it, or I knew you wouldn't believe me. Don't worry. She should still be unconscious from the tranq dart I put in her..."

Layla had bounded to the far side of the enclosure and was digging under the fence, using all her shifter speed.

Be stubborn, Noah, she said mentally. *Keep arguing.*

She was halfway under the fence, paws churning, dirt flying up behind her.

Grange was intoning his counterspell to remove the spell net.

Layla dug harder.

There was a faint ringing sound as the net overhead fizzled out. They were almost through. Dimly, ears muffled in her tunnel of dirt, she could hear the gate squeak open.

She scrabbled as hard as she could, dirt choking her. Just another foot...six inches...

"Where the fuck is she?"

She was free.

Trish ran full out, across the open grass and into the woods.

Behind her, she heard the curses of an angry lion.

CHAPTER 35

Noah stared around the enclosure at the dead sheep. The coppery scent of blood filled the air, like old pennies.

He couldn't believe Trish had done something like this. But her scent was there, in the center of the enclosure, where Grange said he'd left her.

She'd always been reticent about her wolf, not Changing with the pack, the understanding being that Trish did sometimes have trouble controlling her. She'd had to suppress her for years, after their original pack was killed and Trish was put into the human foster system.

If the Council had known she'd survived the attack, they'd never have let that happen. They were all lucky Trish had never been found out as a shifter.

But for her to do something like this—to tear a couple dozen sheep apart just for fun—he couldn't see it.

Unfortunately, Trish was not there to ask.

Grange, after a bout of truly inventive cursing when he saw how Trish had tunneled out of the enclosure, had gone quiet and thoughtful, rubbing absently at one of the wounds on his arm.

Probably wondering how pissed off Emon was going to be about him having Trish arrested. Sometimes it sucked working for a psycho dragon.

It did look like Trish had chewed up Grange pretty thoroughly—but Noah couldn't see Trish doing that either. Not without a good reason.

Abruptly, Grange said, "You have to go after her."

Noah raised his eyebrows. "Me? Why me? You're probably faster. Not to mention, if I go after her in wolf form, how am I going to drag her back if she doesn't want to come?"

"Well, she's sure as hell not going to let me get near her." Grange gestured to his still-bleeding wounds.

"We need Tristan," Noah said. "If she's out of control, he's probably the only one she'll listen to. Or better yet, Emon. He can find her from the air, and he might be dominant enough to control her, especially if she cares about him. Otherwise I'm going to have to drag Jace here from Silverlake—as her alpha, he can make her obey. But I really don't want to do that except as a last resort. If nothing else, it's a jurisdictional nightmare."

Grange was still rubbing his arm, still with that thoughtful, faraway look on his face. "Right," he said. "Maybe we should just wait until Emon comes back. That'll be late tonight—tomorrow, at the latest. By that time she might have even calmed down and come back on her own."

Maybe. Noah wasn't so sure about that. This was bad trouble, and if Trish was thinking straight, she'd want to wait for Emon too.

This was his territory, and what to do about this mess was ultimately up to him. If he didn't want to press charges, he could make the whole thing go away. Especially if he was willing to keep Trish here under his protection.

Although Noah was still going to have to report it to Jace. He rubbed his hand through his hair and sighed.

"Yeah," Grange said, looking relieved. "That's what we'll do. Wait."

Noah gazed at him, his eyes narrowing. There was something off here. At first Grange was all gung-ho to have Trish arrested and taken back to Silverlake immediately, and now suddenly he'd done a complete about-face.

Noah started to get a hot prickling feeling in his stomach—the one he always got on an Enforcer job when something wasn't right.

He only had Grange's word that Trish had ever been here. Or that she'd caused the wounds on his body. Those were identifiable as wolf bites, but the damage to the sheep was not. They were so torn apart it was impossible to tell what kind of animal had done the damage.

Had Grange done something to Trish? Attacked her and gotten the worst of it, and then torn apart the sheep and blamed Trish to make her look out of control?

But then why would he suddenly want to wait for Emon to come back?

None of this made any fucking sense.

He followed Grange back to the castle, mind whirring. He didn't like the smell of this situation at all.

As they entered the castle through one of the side doors, he asked Grange, "Is Mayah in her room?"

Grange shrugged. "I guess. It's where she usually is." Then he frowned. "Why?"

Noah said, "I know Emon left you in command, but legally, with him gone, Mayah's in charge of the domain. I'd like to run this by her and see what she says."

And also see what she had to say about Grange. And what Tristan and Brock had to say as well. Come to think of it, Brock had never really been friendly with Grange. He was more friendly to Emon, who was certifiably nuts, than he was to the normal-seeming lion.

And Brock had an uncanny way of seeing into people's minds—and hearts.

He started up the stairs, and heard behind him, "I'm afraid I can't let you do that." Then a jolt of electricity froze his entire body, and he was gone.

Grange looked down at the Enforcer lying in the hallway. Luckily, there were no staff around to see him—they were all snoozing in the staff dining room, courtesy of one of Ragnor's special recipes.

The Al-Maddeiri princess was subdued and collared, unable to Change or use her powers. Tristan, Mina and Brock were locked in Mayah's room with her, a powerful spell net keeping them there.

Trish and Noah had been the last loose ends. He'd set her up so that Noah would have to take her back to

Silverlake, getting rid of him too. That hadn't worked out, but if she thought she'd really killed all those sheep and attacked Grange, then she'd be too afraid to come back.

Even if she did realize she'd been set up, she still wouldn't come back. She'd probably try to go find Emon. That would take a while. Long enough for Grange to do what he needed to do.

Yes, this would work just as well. He'd get rid of the Enforcer, and if Emon started back too soon, he could divert him on a search for Trish.

Everything was still on track. He was almost there.

Grange slung Noah's inert form over his shoulder, and carried him off to dispose of him.

When he was done, he took the King's Key up to the huge empty laboratory where Ragnor used to do his experiments on the prince and princess. Where Trish had almost caught him after she'd found him in Ragnor's study.

He'd already done everything Gen-X had asked of him. He'd captured the white wolf, the princess, and the little boy with the strange mental powers.

He'd used the King's Key to unlock Ragnor's study. He was ready.

He got out his private communicator and put in the call to Earth. "Everything's set," he said. "I'll be activating the portal momentarily."

"Copy that. Good work."

Grange held the King's Key in both hands and

opened the portal that would lead him to freedom—and wealth beyond all his imaginings.

CHAPTER 36

Emon stood at the entrance to the iron mine. It was not more than a couple of hours past noon, and already he was anxious to get back.

Digging out the mine had ended up being much more difficult than they'd thought. It turned out that there were, in fact, people trapped down there—a small team doing an unscheduled inspection before the shift started.

No one seemed to know what had triggered the collapse. There was no sign of instability in the surrounding area, that anyone had been able to find.

Luckily, no one had been injured or killed, but digging down to them had turned out to be slow and arduous, even with his dragon doing most of the heavy lifting. They'd had to shore up the collapsed tunnel with supports every few feet, and that took time.

He wished to hell he had his magic—things would have gone a lot faster. But it had nearly deserted him in the last few days, as his wound got worse.

Finally they were on the verge of reaching the trapped workers, and he'd gotten his huge bulk out of the way, letting the humans tunnel through the last few yards.

After this, he'd just have to clear the road, and then he would be able to head back.

He stretched gingerly, trying to ease the pain in his side. Oddly enough, the heavy work had seemed to help. Or maybe it just took his mind off the pain.

But it was kind of nice to be needed. It felt—right.

A cheer went up as the rescue group came out of the mine, tired and dusty, but escorting the three miners who'd been trapped. They were instantly surrounded by friends and loved ones, faces full of relief and tears.

At least someone was getting a happy ending.

The mine manager was talking to the men, gesturing towards Emon. Obviously, that was his cue to go over and shake their hands, accept their thank-yous, make all the right noises.

But he was bone-tired. Soul-tired. Could he get away with being grumpy and standoffish, and not accepting thanks? The aloof Lord of the Draken?

Because not having to talk to anyone would be pretty welcome right about now.

The mine manager was looking hopefully at him. Right. Everyone wanted to meet the Darkwing Dragon, who, to their surprise, had turned out to be somewhat friendly and had not eaten even one person.

But before he could take a step, a voice echoed faintly in the back of his head. *Emon? Emon, can you hear us?*

Mayah?

Kind of. It wasn't, though. This had an echo of

Mayah's mental voice, but it wasn't her. And they'd never been able to communicate from this far away.

The mine manager was walking toward him. Emon put up a hand sharply, stopping the man in his tracks. He turned away, blocking out everything else.

Who is this? Emon demanded.

It's Tristan. Mayah and Brock are boosting the signal.

Emon hadn't even known that was possible. *Is Mayah all right?*

For the moment, Tristan said. *But I think we're under attack.*

Fire blazed through Emon. *Who? Who dares?* His voice thundered through the connection.

We don't know. Early this morning, Mayah had another one of her nightmares. Mina, Brock and I came to help her. While we were here, someone locked us in her room and sealed it with a spell. And they'd put some kind of collar on her, too—she can't Change, or use any of her powers.

Emon closed his eyes and breathed deeply. His dragon wanted to bust out right now and start flaming things—anything—but he had to stay calm.

It wasn't a military attack, or they'd be dead. And they'd have heard shots. Had the person looking for Ragnor's research finally made his move?

What about everyone else? he asked. *Trish? Noah? Grange? The staff?*

We don't know, Tristan said again. *They're not with us.*

At least no one's hurt, Emon said. He had to hold on to that.

So far, Tristan said. He paused, then added, *I'd like*

for you to keep thinking that's a good thing, but…this isn't the first time someone's tried to get their hands on Brock and me. Because of our special abilities. And a dragon—especially an Al-Maddeiri dragon…

He trailed off, but he didn't need to finish.

Cages. Experiments. Fucking Gen-X. It was going to start all over again. Someone was going to try to take his sister away, and Brock and Tristan with her.

Taking care of his sister was the only thing Emon had never failed at. He couldn't fail her now.

I'm coming, he said. *Hang on.*

He waved the mine manager over and told him there was an emergency at the castle. "I'll be back as soon as I can to clear the road."

Without waiting for a reply, he ran a few steps to give himself room, burst into dragon form, and launched himself into the sky.

As he flew, he called out to Trish. He knew it was stupid; they'd only ever talked mind-to-mind when they were right next to each other. The chances of her hearing him at this distance and being able to project her thoughts back to him were less than zero.

But he had to try.

Mayah and Tristan and Brock were valuable targets. Trish was not. If this was Gen-X, or someone like them, Trish would be nothing but collateral damage to them.

Trish! he called out, as loudly as he could. *Layla! Trish! Can you hear me?*

And he flew faster than he ever had before.

Trish, still in wolf form, was streaking across the plains toward the atherias mine. The red dragons had a communicator. She could use it to call Emon.

Because if Grange was setting her up, trying to get rid of her, then he was the one who'd been behind all the strange happenings in the castle.

He was the one who'd broken into Ragnor's office, and set up the theft from Emon's hoard so that the research team would be blamed.

Which meant he was either in league with Gen-X, or he wanted Ragnor's research for himself, to use or sell.

And that meant everyone in the castle was in danger. Gen-X was capable of anything—and they'd love to get their hands on a white wolf. Tristan. Brave, loyal Tristan. And Brock. She couldn't let anything happen to them.

Then go back and kill, Layla growled.

Not yet. We need the Darkwing Dragon.

As if in answer, Trish heard a faint voice in her mind, calling out.

Trish? Layla? Can you hear me? Trish!

Emon! He sounded desperate, almost pleading. They stopped, ears pricked, scanning the sky. *We're here!*

Trish tried to project a picture of her surroundings, including the mountains, so he'd know where she was.

Layla tipped her head back and let out a howl.

Within a few minutes, she saw a black dot in the sky, moving fast. She kept howling. *We're here!*

The dragon grew larger, flying directly toward her like she was a homing beacon. He swooped in and back-winged to slow himself down, then Changed before his feet even hit the ground.

He was covered in grit and dust, and he'd never looked so beautiful.

"Layla!" he said breathlessly, running over to her. "What are you doing out here? Are you okay?"

We are fine.

"What's going on at the castle?"

Layla went silent. Trish tried to Change, but Layla wouldn't let her.

Emon went on, "Tristan contacted me and said that someone imprisoned him and Brock and Mayah and Mina in Mayah's room. They don't know what happened to Grange or Noah. We're thinking that Gen-X must have somehow found a way in. I need to know what's going on. And who's behind it."

Lion-man, Layla said, growling. Trish could feel the darkness building inside her.

"Grange?" Emon asked, sounding unable to believe it.

Layla growled louder. *Said we did bad things. We didn't. Must kill him.*

Trish pressed against her, trying to Change, but Layla held her ground.

"Fuck," Emon said. "I need to talk to Trish."

Layla backed up. *NO. We need to fight. I fight. She does not.*

"First I need to talk to her." He was putting out his alpha juice, and Layla pushed back. Trish could feel her bracing herself to defy Emon's authority.

But instead of insisting, Emon dropped the alpha posture and stepped forward, hands out. "Please."

His eyes met Layla's.

After a moment her head dipped, and she let Trish have her body. But she stayed in the back of her head, watching and listening.

Emon gathered Trish into his arms. "Are you okay?"

She took a deep breath, hugging him back, but she didn't let herself sag against him. "I'm fine," she said. "I don't suppose you can make me some clothes?"

Immediately she was dressed—in armored leather. "Tell me what happened this morning," he said.

Trish told him the story of Grange and the sheep. "He set me up," she said. "I just don't know why."

"To get you and Noah out of the way," he answered. "Just like he got me out of the way. That mountain was stable. That mine was stable. He must have rigged an explosion—"

"But how?" she interrupted. "He hasn't left the castle since I've been here."

"He must have made a portal," Emon murmured, half to himself. "The King's Key, maybe. If he found it, he can make the portals go anywhere. The mine. The Dragonlands. Earth."

"Gen-X," Trish added. "Do you think he's been in with them all along?"

Emon shook his head. "Don't know. Don't care. All I know is I have to get back there before he tries to hand Mayah and the others over to whoever he *is* working for. And then I have to kill him."

"I'm coming too," Trish said immediately. When he hesitated, she added, "Those are my friends back there. My pack. A little boy, for fuck's sake. If you think for one minute that I'm not going to fight for them—"

Yes, Layla said. *Good shifter. Fight.* And then spoiled it by adding, *Finally.*

CHAPTER 37

Emon flew in from the south, cloaked, but staying low behind the trees anyway in case Grange had some way of detecting him. He put Trish down by the portal entrance leading back to Silverlake.

"Keep that communicator," he said, indicating the one he'd given her before he flew them back here. "I'll get the spare out of my jacket." A jacket appeared on him, and he reached into the pocket, coming out with a golden ball.

"Nice trick, Draken Prince."

He said, "Your communicator will open the portal—it's keyed to the House of Al-Maddeiri. Just hold it up to the hand plate."

"What? I'm not going through the portal. I'm going with you."

"I need you to get backup from Silverlake," he said. "Who the hell knows how many people Grange might have in there by now. I may be a dragon, but once I'm inside I have to go human, and there's only one of me."

She opened her mouth to protest, and he said again, "Please. I need you to bring the Enforcers."

"I'd rather bring Kira."

"So would I, but we already tried that." She'd tried to reach Kira on the way, while he was flying, but there had been no answer. Her communicator was probably in a drawer somewhere in the Bad Blood territory.

Emon cupped Trish's chin in his hand. "I'm counting on you."

"Be safe," she whispered. "And flame their sorry asses."

"Will do."

He gave her a hard kiss, and then he Changed and took off for the castle, winking out of sight as he cloaked himself.

Trish took a step toward the panel that opened the portal, set into a rock formation. Then she stopped, pressing her lips together. This was just wrong. The Enforcers couldn't get mustered and get here in time to do anything. She was just running away.

Yes, Layla said. *Do not go. Fight.*

We still need backup.

We need no one.

They did need people. But there was someone closer than Silverlake she could call. Three someones.

She gripped the communicator in her hand, and said, "Zakerek."

There was a humming sound and a musical chime, and then Zakerek's face appeared in the communicator.

Holy hell. It worked.

"What do you want, my esteemed and worshipful prince?" he asked. Then he got a good look at who was calling.

"Oh," he said. "What do *you* want?"

"Your esteemed and worshipful prince is in danger," she said. "And your princess. They need your help." She filled them in on the situation as best she could.

"And we should help them why?" Zakerek asked. "Because he enslaved us? And he gives us such nice things?"

"Because he didn't kill you, even though you worked for Ragnor and fought against Emon?"

"Oh, yay, I'm not dead. So grateful."

"Or because you want to be a clan. Because you want him to lead you."

"I certainly do not," Zakerek said. "Yechh."

Behind him she could see parts of Cazbek and Mikah, who had come up behind him and were listening in. "But you do," she said, looking past Zakerek to Mikah. "I think you all do. And I think you're right, Emon needs a clan. What better way to say 'I love you and I want to be in your clan' then fighting on his side and helping him save his sister?"

"I don't want to say 'I love you'," Zakerek said. "Maybe he'll die, and the mine will be all ours. And the castle, too."

"And maybe Mayah will die, and you'll feel even more shitty about yourself than you already do."

"Not possible. Hard pass on the rescue mission."

"Fine," she said. "I'm going. Here I go, throwing my life away for the people I care about. Because that's what decent people do."

"I won't cry at your funeral. But if there's cake, maybe I'll come."

"Fine. Come to the rescue or don't. I'm going."

And she cut the connection.

She should have gone to Silverlake. Maybe she should still go.

But every instinct told her that Emon needed her. And he needed her now.

She heard a huge dragon roar from the roof of the castle, and she began to run. At the castle's foundation was the tunnel that Flynn, Kira, Sloan and Caitlyn had used to sneak in when they rescued Emon and Mayah.

It was locked, a huge stone covering the entrance, but the lock, like everything else, was keyed to the blood of Al-Maddeiri. Trish pressed the communicator against it and the stone slid open.

Now it was time to run fast and silent. Trish called on her wolf. Not in fear, but gladly. Gratefully. *Layla, I need you. We need to do this together.*

And Layla came. Not the darkness that took her over, that pushed Trish out of the way. Her partner. Together, they were the Nightmare Wolf. And Emon and the Darkwing Dragon needed them.

CHAPTER 38

There were two guards on the roof. Gen-X, it looked like, because they were wearing Earth-style military tactical equipment and carrying Earth weapons.

Long-range rifles, which were not that much of a problem for Emon. And some kind of big gun like a grenade launcher, which might be.

And special vision scopes that saw right through his cloak. In seconds, both weapons were trained on him.

Rather than trying to dodge, he just folded his wings and dove, breathing fire. They scattered, getting off a few rounds before they made cover. One rifle bullet hit Emon in the flank, but he barely felt it.

<*Kill them*> his dragon said.

On it.

He strafed the roof with fire, catching the rifleman, who screamed as his uniform erupted in flames. The other guard had a magical heat shield. He aimed his launcher at Emon.

He couldn't get out of the way in time. But instead of being hit by a grenade, it was some kind of spear gun, the spear sticking in his back next to his spine. Fuck. A toxin?

The spear broke off and fell to the ground, but he could feel part of the point sticking in his skin, burrowing inside.

He landed on the roof, sweeping his tail around and slamming the shooter into the parapet. He crumpled, unconscious.

And then Emon felt a shudder run through him, and suddenly he was human. His dragon roared, thrashing inside him, but he couldn't get out. He reached for his magic, and couldn't find it.

Fuck. Whatever was sticking in his back was some kind of inhibitor—and it must have been made specifically for dragons. Unfortunately the shot had been perfect—it was right where he couldn't reach it.

Fine. Emon picked up the spear gun and threw it over the parapet. The rifle he kept. There was more than one way to deal with Gen-X.

Emon started down the stairs, his mind whirring.

If Grange had the King's Key, he could make a portal *to* anywhere. But because of the way the castle was constructed, there were only a few places inside where a portal could be created, regardless of where it came from or where it went.

Limited portal access cut down on the invasions—but apparently, not enough.

The closest portal-friendly area was Ragnor's old lab. He'd head there first.

There were four guards on the balcony that circled the lab, two on each side. Emon sneaked up behind the nearest one. It would have been a lot easier if he were cloaked, but that damn thing sticking in his back kept him from using any of his powers.

Luckily, he and Mayah had spent their childhood playing Draken Wars and sneaking up on each other in this castle. He knew all the hiding places, and all the tricks.

He sprang at the first guard and got him in a choke hold, cutting off his air. The man sank silently to the ground, Emon grabbing his weapon before it could make a clatter on the stone.

One down. He dragged the body off into the shadows and took his combat vest and helmet. From a distance, he'd look just like all the other guards.

The combat vest held spare ammo, flashbangs, and grenades. Nylon rope and a grappling hook, a knife, a few other goodies. Not as good as fire and lightning, but it would have to do.

He crept along the edge of the balcony, checking out the other guards. They were all splitting their attention between the entrances to the balcony, and what was going on below.

He could still see a shimmer of magic where a portal had been, but it was closed now. Temporary portals were one-way, so they had to shut it down before they could open another one to go back where they came from.

Near the portal was a large rolling cart, half-full of boxes. Several men in combat gear were carrying more boxes out of Ragnor's study and stacking them on top of the others.

Fucking shit on piece of toast. They were cleaning out Ragnor's research. All of it. He could not let that happen.

He started counting soldiers. Three up here. At least one outside the main door, by the staircase. Probably two. Four men standing guard inside on the main level, at least three carrying boxes. Grange, wherever the hell he was.

A minimum of thirteen enemy combatants, maybe more. And him with one rifle, no dragonfire, and no magic.

The odds didn't look good.

And then it got worse. From one of the side doors, two more soldiers led out Mayah, Tristan, Brock and Mina. They were all bound in some kind of rope that glowed faintly in the dim light. Something else that probably inhibited magic, or mind powers, or both. Mayah had on a thick necklace he'd never seen before.

The collar Tristan had told him about. Like his inhibitor, it would bind her magic and her innate Draken powers.

Grange came out of Ragnor's study, along with the most average, nondescript man Emon had ever seen. Brown hair, average height, average build, average face. Generic black suit. The only thing that stood out was his dark red tie.

Sixteen men, now. It was all Emon could do to keep from growling. They'd dared to touch his people. They were all going to die.

He just had to figure out how.

Trish raced through the darkened castle on four legs, a silent shadow. Up from the dungeons, into the Great Hall and up the main staircase, staying against the wall so she was harder to see.

She could feel Emon somewhere above her. He'd told her where internal portals could be opened, and she was heading for the closest one to the roof.

Praying Emon had gotten in without getting hurt. And that they could get the others out.

Were the red dragons coming? Would they get here in time?

It didn't matter. Emon was her mate, the only one for her. Her place was by his side. Win or lose, fight or die. She didn't want to be safe, if it meant being without him.

There were guards at the top of the stairs—she could smell them. Humans, two of them, with guns, near the entrance to Ragnor's old lab—the huge room at the top of the stairs, where Grange had escaped to after she'd caught him searching the study.

Where Emon had kissed her.

Where I bit him, Layla said. *Hard.*

How about biting some enemies from Gen-X? Really, really hard?

Yes. Hunt. Kill.

For once, Trish was okay with that.

She crouched on the stairs, listening intently. There were more men inside, lots of them, lots of smells. Too many. Where was Emon?

Then she heard a voice among the small murmurs and noises of footsteps and things moving—a human voice she didn't recognize.

"So here they are. The Al-Maddeiri princess, the white wolf, and the miraculous little boy I've heard so much about."

"Stay away from him." Mina's voice. Trish's ears pricked up. All four of them were in there. But where was Emon?

"You won't get away with this, Johnson," Tristan said. "Our people will find us, wherever we are. And they'll take you down."

"Brave words, white wolf." The voice was calm, controlled. "But abominations like you can't be loose in the world. Too much power, too little control."

"Oh, and you're making the world safe for everyone?"

"Safe for humans," he said. He raised his voice, clearly talking to someone else. "Are we about through in there?"

The man talking was a stranger to Trish, but the man who answered wasn't.

Grange. Fucking traitor.

"Just about. These are the last boxes."

It was all she could do to keep from growling and giving her position away.

"Good. Open the portal. I want to get out of here as soon as possible."

Oh, no fucking way was he taking her friends out of

here. Not if she had to chew her way through every damn soldier in that room.

Trish crept through the shadows, almost to the top of the stairs, and prepared to attack.

CHAPTER 39

From his place on the balcony, Emon watched them load the last boxes onto the cart. He had to wait for just the right moment, when he had the best chance of not getting everyone killed.

Emon?

His heart leaped. It was Trish. *Where are you?*

On the main staircase. Just below the guards.

She was here. She came. She shouldn't be here; he'd sent her to Silverlake to keep her safe. But hope and happiness blossomed inside him, all the same.

I've got your back, she said. *Just tell me what you need.*

Did you find help?

Not here yet, but they're coming. She didn't sound sure, and he didn't have time to wait. He'd never really thought they'd get there in time, anyway. He'd just wanted her out of danger. Now he realized how stupid that was. They belonged together, fighting side by side.

They're about to open the portal, he said. *We have to move.*

Just tell me when.

Grange walked up in front of the portal area, the King's Key in his hand. Fucking traitor. Raiding the hoard had been a diversion; the Key was what he'd wanted. He activated the Key, starting the spell to create the portal.

Emon said to Trish, *Now.*

He aimed his stolen rifle at the King's Key and pulled the trigger, shooting it right out of Grange's hands. He didn't even bother to watch the reaction in the room, just attached the grappling hook to the top of the balustrade and swung himself over.

He slid down the rope, holding it with his legs and one hand, automatic rifle tucked under his free arm, spraying the guards between him and the door with a clip of bullets.

As he neared the floor, he yanked the sheathed knife off his combat vest and threw it to Tristan.

Tristan reached his bound hands up and caught it, a feral grin on his face, his eyes glowing gold. As Emon hit the floor, Tristan was already cutting the enspelled ropes around him and the others.

Then the guards opened fire, and everyone dove for cover.

As soon as she heard Emon's '*Now*,' Trish leaped out of the darkness at the nearest guard, throwing him off-balance and sending him tumbling down the stone steps.

Before he'd even hit the bottom, she was on the other one, a nightmare out of the shadows.

All hell was breaking loose inside the room, the rattle of gunfire echoing painfully off the stone. The second guard had a knife, but she tore it ruthlessly out of his hand.

She had to get to Emon; she had to save the others. It was all that mattered. Snarling viciously, Trish and Layla fought as one.

Emon upended a table and ducked behind it, trying to pick off more of Gen-X's soldiers. The King's Key was lying on the floor, and fucking Grange was crawling toward it. Emon didn't have a shot.

"Tristan!" he yelled. "Get Grange!"

Tristan cut through the last bit of rope binding him, and handed the knife off to Mina. Then the white wolf stood up, a look of terrible concentration on his face, and flung his arm out at Grange.

Emon saw a faint flash of energy, and then Grange sank to his knees, holding his head, his face contorted in pain and blood pouring out of his nose.

Holy fuck. Tristan was attacking people with his mind.

He flung his arm out again, this time at one of the guards on the balcony. Good thinking. Keep them from picking him and Tristan off from above.

Emon went back to firing his rifle. He had two objectives—keep his people safe, and out of that damn portal. And keep these fuckers from making off with Ragnor's research.

Out of the corner of his eye, he saw Mina go wolf and attack the nearest guard. Never fuck with a mother and her kid.

Brock was still cutting himself and Mayah free.

Emon shot and ducked, shot and ducked, trying to keep track of Grange and the guy in the suit. Johnson. They were the leaders—the ones to watch. Everyone else was just muscle.

Johnson had managed to grab the King's Key, and was trying to form a portal.

Emon couldn't get Tristan's attention; he was still trying to take out the guards on the balcony, but he was swaying on his feet. Those mind-blasts were sucking him dry.

Emon ran from behind his table to behind the cart of boxes, trying to get to Johnson before he could finish opening the portal.

Too late, he saw Grange stagger over to Mayah, who Brock had just freed from her bonds. Brock went after him with the knife, but Grange shoved him roughly aside and he hit the wall, sliding to the floor.

Grange pinned Mayah's arms and carried her toward Johnson. The portal began to form.

Emon, growling, dashed across the empty space, trying to get to his sister. A bullet smashed into his leg, knocking him to the floor. He felt a rush of warmth, and blood spurted out.

Fuck. An artery. He dragged himself out of the line of fire and pressed on his thigh, howling with rage more than pain. If he moved his hands, he was fucking dead.

Trish burst through the doors into the room, straight into the thick of the fight. Some enemy soldiers were down, but some were still shooting. She pounced on one, teeth bared, and took him out before he even realized she was there.

Grange was carrying a struggling Mayah toward a quickly forming portal. Mayah head-butted him and he staggered, losing his hold on her. Mayah twisted free, and Tristan tossed her a rifle. She swung it around, slamming the butt into the side of Grange's head. He went down.

Mayah ducked behind a table and began shooting.

But where was Emon?

Trish scanned the room. He was on the floor, blood pouring from a wound on his leg and pooling on the floor.

Emon!

I'm okay he said. *Get Johnson. The suit. We have to keep that portal closed.*

But he wasn't okay. He was bleeding out—she could feel his energy draining away.

Not Emon! No!

There's nothing you can do for me. Mayah was trying to get to him, but she was pinned down by rifle fire. No one else was close enough.

The portal was forming.

Emon was dying.

Get Johnson. You can't help me.

Fuck that shit.

She bounded over to Emon as if there were wings on her paws. A bullet cut through her, and then another, but she barely felt them.

She had to make it.

Trish! Don't!

A third bullet thudded into her, and she stumbled. Darkness hovered, threated to take her, but she fought it as she always had. She hadn't let death get the upper hand all those years, and she wasn't going to do it now.

With the last of her strength, she lunged at Emon and bit him right over the wound. Deep. To the bone.

I claim you. Mate. You are mine.

Blue lightning crackled around them.

Trish felt the lightning jolt through her. Draken blood burned her mouth, her throat, her muscles and nerves, her flesh, her soul.

And then everything stopped. Her heart, her lungs, her blood, her brain. For one terrifying second, she was dead.

Then the energy exploded, healing her wounds, knitting together flesh and bone. She let go of Emon, expecting to see his leg healing. But it wasn't. He was staring at her, eyes dark.

The lightning wasn't surrounding him; the bond wasn't taking. It was slipping off him.

"I can't," he whispered. "My power—it's bound."

And then behind him, she saw Brock, growling, with a knife in his hand. With one quick motion, he stabbed Emon in the back.

CHAPTER 40

Emon felt the knife blade go in. It cut, and twisted, and then small fingers were yanking the inhibitor out of his back.

Lightning crackled around him and Trish, crackled in his veins. Deep inside him, his dragonfire returned.

He was Draken, and magic ran through his veins.

And he was mated. The mating bond encircled him and Trish, making them one, making them whole, making them strong.

It healed the wound in his leg, restoring his lost blood, his lost powers.

He rose to his feet, his wolf-mate at his side, and roared, blasting fire into the air.

He flung a shield spell at the portal just as it finished forming, blocking access. With the other hand, he hit the last soldier in the balcony with lightning, and he fell over the balustrade and landed on the floor.

Then, through the noise and the carnage, a clear, magically amplified voice yelled, "Stop!"

Everyone froze.

Fucking Grange. That lion just did not stay down.

He'd captured Mayah in another spell rope, and

covered them with a magical shield. At her throat was an atherias knife that glowed with magic. Johnson, the coward, stood behind him.

"Open the portal, Al-Maddeiri," Grange snarled. "Johnson and I leave now, or the princess is dead on the floor."

They didn't want to kill Mayah. She was too valuable to them.

"Don't do it, Brother," she called.

But could he take that chance?

"Five seconds," Grange said. "Four. Three. Two…

The wall next to him exploded, and a giant red tail smashed through it, hitting Grange in the back. Mayah kicked backwards, getting him in the balls. And then a huge dragon claw reached through the hole in the wall and grabbed him.

Mikah and Cazbek, in human form, slid down Zakerek's leg and landed on the floor, shooting spell nets as they came. Emon joined them, capturing the rest of the surviving Gen-X operatives.

Suddenly, Emon felt his shield dissolve. He turned just in time to see Johnson dash through the portal.

He raced over there, but the portal shimmered and vanished, and Emon was left pounding the wall where it had been.

Fuck it all. Johnson was the ringleader, the one he really wanted. The man with the average, forgettable face.

But Emon would never forget it. This wasn't over.

For today, though, it was. They'd won the battle. He

and Trish had saved their people—with a little help from their frenemies.

And then Brock looked around, frowning.

"Where's Daddy?"

Mina, still naked from Changing back from wolf, went over to where Grange was lying on the floor, groaning and bleeding.

She smacked his face, hard. "What did you do to Noah, you bastard? If you killed him, I swear to god I'll rip your fucking throat out. Wake up and talk, you motherfucker!"

Before Emon could go over there and dig the information painfully out of his brain, Brock put his hand on Mina's arm. "It's okay, Mommy. I listened with my mind. Noah Gray Woof isn't dead."

Mina closed her eyes, clenching her fist tightly. "Are you sure?"

"Uh huh. I can feel him. He's in the basement. Very down deep."

"The dungeon, probably," Emon said. "We'll get him."

Brock looked down at Grange, growling, his little-boy face as hard and angry as Emon had ever seen it. "I always knew you were a bad man. Now you made me so mad my woof needs to kill a rabbit."

Emon said, "You knew he was bad? You might have told us that."

"I thought he might decide to be good," Brock said. "Sometimes people do. But he stayed bad." He gave another growl, and then said, "Come on, Mommy. Let's get Daddy."

Mayah said, "I'll take them to the dungeon, while you deal with this mess. If someone will *please* get this goddamn collar off me."

It took Emon a minute to figure out how the magic lock worked, but finally he had it off her. Mayah threw the collar on the floor and stomped on it. Then she said, "Come on. Let's go."

Tristan went with them, still looking a bit pale from all the mind magic he'd done.

Trish had Changed back to human, and Emon conjured some clothes for her so she didn't have to walk around naked. Then he looked around at the surviving Gen-X soldiers, lying bound in one corner of the room, their critical wounds tended.

With a sigh, Emon said, "We're going to have to figure out what to do with these guys until we can hand them over to Silverlake."

Trish said dubiously, "They don't really fall under Council jurisdiction; they're human. Except for Grange."

Emon said, "They made war on shifters. That's Council business. And you really don't want *me* deciding what should ultimately be done with them. Because I'm still in a very bad mood."

His dragon said, <Snacks.>

Don't tempt me.

"Well, there's always the dungeon, once we get Noah out," Trish said. "That should hold them."

But Emon noticed she was looking at the three red dragons, all human now, lounging in a corner. "You really should go talk to them," she said. "They did save Mayah's life."

Emon was in no mood for Zakerek, but Trish was right. He owed the Wild Dragons big. He sighed. "I guess I should."

He started to get up, but she put her hand on his arm. "You know, all they really want is somewhere to belong. And I think you need people to belong to you."

Oh, no. He was not going where he thought this was going. "I have you."

"I know. And I get that I'll always be your favorite, because of the sexytimes." She winked at him. "But like it or not, you're a king. And you enjoy running your country. Not to mention that you're good at it. Couldn't you use some more dragony help?"

Emon snorted. "These guys?"

"Well, obviously it's up to you. I'm not going to try to talk you into anything you don't feel is right for your domain. But I do think that maybe you need this. You need a purpose in life, people to take care of."

No, he didn't. Did he?

"You really think I should form a clan?"

"I think you should think about it."

He sighed again.

Mikah and Cazbek shook his hand and accepted his thanks. Zakerek just stood with his arms folded, glowering.

Even after Emon broached the possibility of forming a clan.

"You all came when my mate called," he said. "You fought for me and the princess. And according to the laws of this domain, which I get to make up, that means your punishment is rescinded and you're pardoned for past crimes." He paused. "At least, the ones I know about."

Zakerek snorted.

"And since I'm thinking about starting a clan of my own, that would make you eligible for membership."

"Why would I want to be in your clan?" Zakerek snapped. "I don't even want to talk to you once a month, when you come out to the mine."

"Well, nobody's going to make you," Emon said. "Think it over."

Zakerek frowned. "Would we have to live in the castle?"

Mikah elbowed him. "We *want* to live in the castle, moron."

This fucking dragon was a piece of work.

Emon shrugged. "You can stay out in your camp if you want. Because it's so nice there. I can see why you wouldn't want to live here, what with the chef and the comfy couches and the hot and cold running water. I'm thinking about opening a permanent portal to Earth, too, so we can have internet."

"What's internet?"

Emon clapped Zakerek on the shoulder. "Trust me. You'll like it. It has porn."

"What's porn?"

CHAPTER 41

Tempest tried to keep her feet as Tyr let go of her and sent a blast of magic at Two weeks later, Trish was being led by Emon through their rooms in the castle, her hands over her eyes.

"Can I look yet?"

"Not yet. I want you to get the full effect."

"But I want my surprise."

"You're going to get many surprises tonight, trust me." Trish felt a familiar shiver run down her spine and blossom between her legs.

She still had the sexiest mate in the entire universe, and she couldn't wait to get her hands on him.

"Okay, open."

Their bedroom was full of flowers. A riot of color, mostly ones she didn't recognize. They were gorgeous, their scents blending to form a rich, sensual perfume.

On a table by the bed was a plate of fruit dipped in chocolate, Trish's favorite cheese, and a decanter of akhasa mead with two goblets made of atherias.

Best yet, all the bloody battle tapestries were gone. Replaced by...

Voluptuous goddesses and muscle-bound gods. All

naked, most of them having sex with someone. Sometimes several someones. They didn't seem picky—they were doing the nasty with each other, with humans, and Trish saw something going on in the corner with a unicorn that she really didn't want to look too closely at.

She bit her lips. Emon's mouth was twitching. Trish gave up being polite and burst out laughing.

"Where in the hell did you get these? They're perverted."

"I know. Aren't they awesome? They were in one of the other rooms."

"Is this decorating choice, um, permanent? Or is there room for negotiation here?"

"I was thinking we could keep them until we'd tried all the things in the pictures."

"Not the group thingies—not my jam. And whatever is going on with that unicorn, I want no part of it. Otherwise, I'm in." Because there were a god and goddess over the dresser doing something that looked like fun, assuming it turned out to be physically possible.

It had been a busy two weeks. Emon had officially petitioned Jace to release Trish from the Silverlake pack, so she could be recognized as part of his new clan. The Wild Dragons were in the process of getting settled into their own wing of the castle.

They'd thrown a big barbecue and invited the Bad Bloods, and their friends from Silverlake, and the Greystone brothers and their mates—Wild Dragons from Earth.

Emon and Thorne Greystone had struck up a friendship and were deep in ongoing discussions of magical security systems and spells. Since Johnson had made off with the King's Key, Emon had to revamp all of the domain's wards and defenses.

Now, as they sat in bed, Emon told her that Thorne had even offered a secure location in his compound for Emon to create a permanent portal between here and Earth.

"So we can get internet," Emon said, topping up her glass of mead. "Thorne even says we can piggyback off their TV."

Trish gasped and clutched her chest dramatically. "Network TV? Be still my heart."

Emon smiled and took a sip of mead. "So are you happy?" he asked quietly.

She kissed a drop of mead off his lips. "Happier than I ever thought I could be. Your wound is healing. We have a clan. Layla is speaking to me. You've given me everything I've ever wanted." She kissed him again, and then whispered against his lips, "Except for the sex dungeon."

"Aaagh," he groaned. "Now look what you've done. You *know* what happens when you say 'sex dungeon' to me."

"Why, no," she said innocently, batting her eyes at him. "What happens?"

"A huge. Giant. Boner." He kissed her in between each word.

"Can I see it?"

"Sure. Do you want me to disappear the pants, or would you rather unwrap it yourself?"

"You know I like to do it."

A slow, sexy smile curved across Emon's face as he stood up. She loved that smile so much; she loved being able to bring it to his face. She put down her mead and wriggled over on her stomach to where he was standing at the edge of the bed.

She unbuttoned his pants and slowly pulled his zipper down. Just an inch.

She could see the tip of his cock, glistening with moisture. Slowly, she licked it. He tipped his head back and moaned.

She moved his zipper down inch by inch, licking his shaft and his head with exquisite slowness. "You're killing me, woman," he murmured.

She pulled the zipper all the way down and wrapped one hand around him, taking him into her mouth, in and out, slow and languid, loving the way he groaned and fisted his hands in her hair.

She sucked on him, swirling her tongue, feeling him beginning to lose control.

Just before he reached the edge, he took a deep breath, then released her and pulled away.

Before she knew what was happening, he'd pulled her up off the bed and flipped her around so she was bent over the edge of the bed, feet on the floor and ass in the air.

He put his hand in the middle of her back and said, "I heard wolves like it from behind. In chains."

He muttered a spell under his breath, and suddenly her wrists were encased in padded shackles, the chains running to the corners of the bed.

She got a rush of heat and wetness.

Holy fuck. It was an instant magical sex dungeon.

Emon bent over and whispered in her ear, "I always keep my promises. And by the way, I'm not the kind of guy who falls asleep after a blow job without the girl getting even a teeny, weeny little orgasm. Because that would be rude."

He reached around her, one hand in front, one underneath, and began stroking her slit, circling her clit, teasing it, rubbing slowly up and down until she was rolling her hips back and forth, moaning.

The chains kept her bent over, pinned to the bed, arms extended in front of her. Emon was totally in control—and totally driving her to insanity.

"Please," she murmured. "Inside me."

She meant his dick, that gorgeous hard as steel shaft that she *needed* inside her. But he slid his fingers up inside her instead, pushing slowly in and out, still teasing her clit with the other hand.

Trish felt her orgasm bearing down on her like a freight train. Emon sensed it, so attuned to her, and gradually increased the pace, pushing her over the edge while she cried out with total abandon.

Before she'd even begun to recover he entered her with his cock, one hard deep thrust after another. He drove into her, a growl rumbling in his chest, as he took her to the brink again.

She felt her wolf rising up in her with a howl and she gave way to her primal urgings, meeting him thrust for thrust, helpless against the intense tide of pleasure.

Just as she was reaching the peak, the chains disappeared, and Emon flipped her over and picked her up as if she weighed no more than a feather. He held her to his chest, and she wrapped her arms and legs around him as he sheathed himself in her and launched them both into the final wave of ecstasy.

She came apart in his arms, and felt him shaking with pleasure and emotion, holding her strong as his dick throbbed and pulsed, emptying himself into her.

He covered her neck and chest with kisses, murmuring love-words, running one hand through her hair the way he loved to do.

"I love you beyond words, Night Wolf," he said. "You are my shining star, the one perfect thing in my life."

"I love you, Darkwing Dragon. Forever and always, as long as a dragon lives, and more."

A Note from Anastasia: Thank you for reading *Dark Dragon's Mate!* I hope you love my sexy Darkwing Dragon as much as I do.

I so, so appreciate all the support from my amazing readers. If you loved Emon and Trish, I would love it if you'd leave a review so other readers like you will know it's the kind of book they like!

And I guess it's obvious whose book is coming next!

Tristan and Mayah get their story in the next book in the series – Dark Dragon's Wolf!

You can also read more about Kane and Rachelle in my **Silverlake Shifters** and **Silverlake Enforcers** series.

And if you want to know more about Kira and Flynn and their crew, check out my **Bad Blood Shifters Series**!

Here's a list of all my books in reading order:

Silverlake Shifters:
Fugitive Mate
White Wolf Mate
Tiger Mate

Silverlake Enforcers:
The Enforcers: KANE

The Enforcers: ISRAEL
The Enforcers: NOAH

Bad Blood Shifters:
Bad Blood Bear
Bad Blood Wolf
Bad Blood Leopard
Bad Blood Panther
Bad Blood Alpha

Wild Dragons:
Dragon's Rogue
Dragon's Rebel
Dragon's Storm

Darkwing Dragons:
Dark Dragon's Mate
Dark Dragon's Wolf

ABOUT THE AUTHOR

Anastasia Wilde lives in the deep forests of the Pacific Northwest, where sexy shifters may or may not be found hiding among the tall, ancient trees. She writes hot paranormal romances about wild, passionate shifter men and the strong women who are destined to win their hearts. Broken, complicated, devoted, protective — love heals their wounds and smooths their rough edges (but not too much!). When not writing, Anastasia is traveling, nomming on any food involving bacon or melty cheese (ideally both), adding to her magical crystal collection, or relaxing with a glass of wine, watching the sun set behind the mountains.

Made in the USA
Monee, IL
17 September 2019